Technically Dead
William Meisel

NSA was facing some of the most difficult challenges in computer science, protecting the nation from both breaches in security and cyber-terrorism, allowing him to do work he felt more challenging and critical than most academic work.

Archie couldn't and didn't talk much about what he accomplished at NSA, but Nikki gathered that his contributions were substantial. With most of his ideas having been implemented within the US security system, Archie saw that US commercial operations were vulnerable to similar attacks from abroad, some sponsored by governments or gangs with substantial resources. He left NSA and joined a commercial firm that helped companies defend their data and computing infrastructure.

Again, he was successful. His skills were more publicly known in this environment, since his company allowed him to present some of his basic methodology and findings at conferences—such publicity brought credibility and business to the company. He became even better known when those presentations led to a request for him to address a Congressional committee trying to understand the changing landscape of international rivalry. Archie's warnings and predictions to the committee made headline news.

Archie had explained that the boundary between warfare and industrial economic competition was becoming blurred. At the beginning of the 21st century, it was largely assumed that China and India would become economic powers challenging the dominance of the US in particular, largely because of the size of their population providing low-cost labor and a local market. But the rapid growth of computer power, "artificial intelligence" technology, and the associated advances in robotics was taking away the labor advantage of developing countries. Robots and AI

4

were doing jobs that previously required human skills, even sewing clothes. US companies were benefiting from this trend, able to compete in manufacturing again. And, even in service industries, where jobs like outsourcing customer service phone calls had been going to countries like India, AI was able to automate most of those jobs. Since scale was a large determinant of efficiency in information technology, particularly with "cloud computing" over the Internet becoming the norm, large US companies had an advantage. Much of AI research that dealt with understanding human language—such as customer service automation—was initially done in English, another advantage for English-speaking countries.

This was creating a potential crisis for developing countries, Archie explained, since their populations were largely pacified by improving economies and the expectations of those not yet benefiting that they or their children ultimately would. Even in the US, increasing automation was restricting job and income growth. But, in the developing countries, growth was plateauing at much lower average income levels. The result was a potential threat to the stability of these countries, particularly in China and Russia, with their large populations. The problem was generating a partnership between industry and the government in those countries, with espionage and theft of trade secrets part of that partnership. This growing problem was part of why Archie left the NSA, he indicated, since the NSA's charter limited what it could do within the US to protect independent companies. Archie argued that US intelligence agencies were set up for a different kind of warfare, and not suited for addressing unfair economic competition between nations.

This publicity led to another episode in Archie's life. A movie producer hired him as a consultant for a film on cyberwarfare. The film was a hit, and Archie's compensation, partly based on the film's success, made him independently wealthy.

Financial independence let Archie work as a consultant without a company affiliation. A problem at the local Los Angeles police department with hacking of their records and destruction of some of those records brought Archie to a local office. While waiting for a meeting on the issue, he overheard Nikki discussing a case with a colleague. Archie took a quick look at some computer files from the case with the help of Erasmus, and this lead to the case being solved.

This interaction fascinated Archie, and he volunteered to help Nikki with cases where analysis of computer files might help. In today's world, this was most cases, so Nikki found herself increasingly calling him, to the point he joined her on many cases, coming into the office on a regular schedule when a case was active. Archie felt challenged by the puzzle solving involved in cases, and became more involved in all aspects of a case over time.

Archie's intelligence, magnified by Erasmus, made him a good partner in solving crimes, and Nikki and Archie were typically given the hardest assignments— or at least those most likely to make the news. And Erasmus could help with the most difficult questions during an investigation, partly because Archie had installed a secret connection between Erasmus and the computers and databases of the National Security Agency before he left the Agency's employ. Nikki once asked him if he wasn't concerned about getting in trouble, and he insisted that all traces of the illegal conduit would disappear if anyone other than him connected with it.

Archie was apparently interested in Nikki as a woman as well as a partner, and this may have partly

motivated his working with her. But Nikki didn't want to develop that aspect of their relationship. Archie was physically attractive, but she didn't want to complicate their professional association. And Archie's lack of social skills could potentially be hard to deal with on a personal level if a relationship went too far. It would be difficult to bring him into a social situation with friends without the likelihood of embarrassment.

He'd recently made his interest in her obvious in his way. It was a conversation after she'd made the mistake of telling him she had been out late on a date the night before, explaining a yawn. They were driving to police headquarters to interview a suspect.

"So, did you have sex?" Archibald asked.

"Archie, I'm not going to give you a blow-by-blow description of my date," she said. "Why are you so curious?"

"I don't like to think about you with other men."

"What?! You sound like a jealous lover!"

"Maybe jealous, but you know I'm not your lover."

"Are you saying you'd like to be?" She wondered how far he'd go with this; a bit worried to hear the answer, but also intrigued. He'd given indications of an interest in her as a women, but not overtly pursued it.

"It would be quite natural for me to want to have sex with you and spend more time with you. You're attractive and smart."

She almost hit the car in front of her as it came to a stop in slow traffic. "Are you propositioning me?"

"I'd like to make love to you. Then you could decide if you wanted to do it again."

The car ahead moved away, but Nicki didn't move until the car behind honked. "Archibald, that's not the way to ask a woman on a date."

"I guess not. I haven't had much time to develop long-term relationships, or interest in doing so. But, of course, like any man, I'm interesting in sexual relations, but don't want to invest much time in maintaining a relationship. I studied sex, and I'm pretty good at it, so some women will go out with me more than once for the sex."

"You studied sex? Don't you need a woman to do that?"

"Well, in high school, a girl named Doris and I practiced together. She said she liked me, that smart was sexy. We got pretty good at it. By the time I went off to college, Doris said she was 'spoiled' and would have a hard time finding someone else as much fun to practice with."

Nicki smiled. "Archibald, you make a compelling case for 'practicing,' but I think it might interfere with our working together."

"Is it OK if I occasionally think about it?"

"If I'm not around when you do."

Mercifully, they had arrived back at headquarters.

Chapter 2

Nikki and Archie arrived at the crime scene after the technician had already begun documenting the evidence. The victim was Edward Hoskins. He was killed in his home. Hoskins had been shot once in his abdomen and there was a lot of blood. The technician said that there was no gun at the scene. The body had been discovered by the housekeeper, who had a key to the house because she often arrived after Hoskins had left.

Nikki looked around. "By the blood trail," she said, "he was alive after the shot and tried to crawl toward the side table. His smartphone is on the table, so perhaps he was trying to call 9-1-1." Archie looked at the table and opened the small drawer, using a gloved hand. There was nothing in the drawer.

Archie thought a moment. "I wonder why the killer left Hoskins alive. Why wasn't there a second shot?"

Nikki thought for a moment. "I guess the killer could have run out of ammo, but that would make him or her a pretty unprepared villain. Perhaps Hoskins faked death or unconsciousness and the killer panicked and ran, afraid someone had heard the shot."

Archie raised his smartwatch. "Erasmus, what do you know about Edward Hoskins of Beverly Hills, California?"

Erasmus acknowledged the request with a slight vibration. After a short pause, he said, "Hoskins is well-known. He founded Involvement.com, a technology company that innovated a product category five years ago. He was about to go public last year to raise money to continue product development, since the company was still losing money. But a competitor announced a product very similar, with some attractive additional features that Hoskins was planning but hadn't yet developed due to a cash shortage. The announcement prevented Hoskins' IPO and eventually led to his company's bankruptcy. The company reportedly had overspent, anticipating the IPO. Interactive Apps, the competitor that caused the problem, bought the assets of Hoskins' company at auction, and was very successful with the product category. That led to Interactive Apps going public, and the founder becoming very wealthy. Hoskins seems on the verge of personal bankruptcy. He is recently divorced. No children. I've sent a detailed report to your cloud storage."

Archie looked puzzled. "That situation might suggest a suicide, but with no gun, that can't be the case."

Nikki said, "And he wouldn't have shot himself in the stomach if it was a suicide. He'd make sure it was quick and painless. Nor would he have crawled toward his phone on the table, presumably to call for help."

Nikki paused in thought. "There is no sign of forced entry, so the killer might have been known to Hoskins. Maybe his soon-to-be ex-wife, for example. Perhaps his calendar will show if he had any planned meetings."

They found a laptop on a desk in a nearby room, a home office. Archie started it up. "Erasmus, can you help with Hoskins' laptop password?"

A vibration signaled that Erasmus was trying. Shortly, he said, "Based on other passwords he has used on websites, I've generated a list of the top ten most likely passwords. See the screen."

Archie tried the ten passwords displayed, but they didn't work. "Erasmus, more candidates." A vibration, then ten more password candidates appeared on the screen of the smartwatch. The second of these worked, and the laptop booted up. Archie commented, "That's a pretty short and simple password for a businessman with a lot of secrets. I guess he didn't trust his memory with a more complex one."

They looked at Hoskins' calendar. There was an entry for earlier that evening: "Tell Michalopoulos what I've got on him."

Archie looked through Hoskins' e-mail contact list and found a George Michalopoulos. "Erasmus, is there a George Michalopoulos associated with Edward Hoskins?"

"George Michalopoulos is the founder and CEO of the company that caused Hoskins to drop the IPO. File sent to the cloud."

Archie turned to Nikki. "If Michalopoulos was here before—or during—the shooting, we have to talk to him."

Nikki said, "The technician can continue to document the crime scene. And I've asked him to check the video surveillance system. We might have a video record of the crime, or at least the criminal leaving."

Archie looked skeptical. "This all seems a bit too easy. I'm sure it won't be that simple."

Chapter 3

Since it was the weekend, they decided to try Michalopoulos' house rather than his office. On the way, Archie studied the documents Erasmus had gathered on his smartphone, summarizing the main points to Nikki as she drove. "Hoskins' company was called Involvement.com. It developed what you might call interactive books. They involved the reader in the story, thus the name of the company. For example, the reader could be part of a detective team—sound familiar?—and be asked to suggest the next step in an investigation. The investigation could continue until the reader identified the murderer. The reader could even interview a suspect. There were also instructional books, from cookbooks to using major consumer software programs, where one could ask a question while listening to or reading informative material."

Archie paused, studying the material. "Interactive books were very expensive to create. The software had to use technology that understood the reader's responses, which could be typed or spoken. Because the story changed depending on the reader's responses, the book required much more content than a standard book, and often took a team to write."

Nikki said, "I can see that. No wonder they weren't profitable, at least at first. Did the books sell well?"

"Involvement.com sold them as a web-based service. Instead of buying the book, you took out a monthly subscription. You could then read as many books as you had time to. Many subscribers would read a book many times to see what changed when their responses were different. The service took off, and had many subscribers.

"But then Michalopoulos launched InteractiveApps.com. He had the same type of content—interactive books—but supported them with ads, without a monthly subscription fee. He also added some semi-pornographic content, sometimes with accompanying video avatars, which drew a new category of users."

Nikki looked puzzled. "How did he get enough interactive content to launch a truly competitive service?"

Archie studied the material Erasmus had provided a moment. "Hoskins apparently hadn't been able to negotiate exclusive deals with most authors. I guess he didn't consider it a priority, as his service became the major outlet for such content, and most authors didn't have a comparable alternative. Michalopoulos was able to simply add much of the content Involvement.com had to his service by offering guaranteed annual royalties to the content providers. Authors were apparently more willing to take deferred payment because they had already received advances from Involvement.com."

Nikki still looked skeptical. "I can see that would provide competition, but I don't see why it would put Hoskins out of business."

"Well, apparently, the competition caused a major drop in subscribers to Hoskins' service, just at a time when he had raised expenditures in anticipation of raising large sums through an IPO. He also chose not to add pornographic content, which garnered him some public support, but the praise didn't result in significant new subscribers. The IPO was delayed, since he had to reflect the drop in subscribers and the new competition in his filing documents."

Archie read further. "That's interesting," followed by silence.

When he didn't continue and seemed absorbed in his reading, Nikki said, "OK, I'll bite. What's interesting?"

"Just as Hoskins' company was adjusting to this challenge, he got a further blow. Hackers hit his website with a denial-of-service attack that delayed responses, and made dealing with an interactive book painfully slow. More subscribers dropped off and went to the competitive site."

He read further. "Wow!" he said, but again nothing followed.

"Archie, are you trying to create suspense? We're almost at Michalopoulos' house."

"Oh," Archie said, as if he had forgotten he was talking to her. "To make matters worse, hackers also stole credit card numbers that had been registered with Involvement.com for the monthly payments. This caused further cancellations, both because users were concerned about security and because the credit card companies issued new credit cards to those subscribers concerned about fraudulent use, invalidating those registered for monthly payments to Involvement.com. Surprisingly, no actual misuse of the credit card information was reported."

"Obviously, this made problems for Involvement.com's going public," Nikki deduced.

"It did," Archie replied. "And it led to the bankruptcy. As I indicated before, the creditors insisted on auctioning off the assets of the company, including patents. Michalopoulos' company bought the assets, including some rights to previously published books and rights to books being developed through advances to authors. This essentially gave them a monopoly on interactive books because of the difficulty in developing the books in quantity. Michalopoulos used the patents aggressively as well, going after any services that offered similar products, whether or not the patents actually applied. Most competitors gave up rather than face the legal costs of fighting the patent cases. His company is now minting money."

"I know about interactive books, of course," Nikki said. "But I've never tried one. Have you?"

"Yes," Archie said. "I like the ones that are essentially structured as a linear story with side trips. For example, a character can mention some episode in their life and, if it sounds interesting, you can say, 'Tell me more.' With those books, the story is essentially one story. Some interactive books have different endings depending on choices by the reader. I guess that tempts you to read it again to find out what would happen if you made different choices, which is interesting, but also time consuming."

"It does sound interesting. E-mail me some recommended reading."

"I will," Archie said. "Economists have commented that the category creates more jobs for creative people, one of the cases where technology creates jobs rather than automating them away. Most of these books actually require a team to write. And standard books can be expanded into interactive books, creating new income for authors."

Chapter 4

They arrived at Michalopoulos' house. It was quite impressive.

Both Archie and Nikki were aware of George Michalopoulos' background; he was a well-known entrepreneur. He was a skilled programmer who started his career working for a technology firm that helped companies with Internet security. He left that company to start a small business on the side, a game for smartphones. It was a simple app that cost less than five dollars to download, but millions of people downloaded it from his website. After his later success, the financial press marveled that he was able to do so well selling the game directly rather than through an app store. But the reported success of the game through this unusual channel led to curiosity among game players, and more sales. The profits, plus proceeds of the sale of the game company to a larger company, were enough to allow Michalopoulos to start his current company without an outside investor.

The company he started, Interactive Apps, was a competitor to Hoskins' Involvement.com. Like Involvement.com, the interactive entertainment was something between a game and a book or video, requiring less activity than a game, but was less passive than a book or video.

When Nikki knocked on Michalopoulos' door, he answered personally. "Can I help you?" he asked.

Nikki said, "Police. We'd like to ask you a few questions about Edward Hoskins."

"OK. I heard about his death while reviewing my morning news briefing. Come in."

They were led into the living room. "How can I help you?" Michalopoulos said after they sat.

"Mr. Michalopoulos," Nikki said. "When was the last time you saw Hoskins?"

Michalopoulos looked uncomfortable. "Unfortunately, last night. I guess that makes me a suspect."

"That remains to be seen," Nikki said cautiously. "Why were you there?"

"He messaged me and asked me to come over. He said he could supply some information I needed to fully use the assets I'd bought from his company. There were some encrypted databases that only he had access to at his company, and he said he wanted to name a price for his giving me passcodes to them. He said he could throw in other information that would help me sort out what was of most value in the assets."

Archie frowned. "Isn't it unusual that he would request a meeting at his house, rather than your office or somewhere more neutral?"

"I said the same thing to him, but he said he wanted to get it over with, that he needed the money, and it was now or never. I was uncomfortable going to his house alone, as he requested, since he's shown his anger toward me on a number of occasions. But I decided to go anyway. He said his lawyer would be there. And, to be honest, I was curious about those databases."

"What time did you arrive at his house?" Nikki asked.

"About 9 PM."

"And what happened when you arrived?"

"He answered the door. I asked where John Taver, his lawyer, was, and he said that he was on his way."

"Is that lawyer John T-A-V-E-R?" Archie asked, touching his smartwatch.

17

"Yes."

Archie looked at the screen of his watch and saw that Erasmus had found the lawyer's office and recorded the information.

Michalopoulos continued. "He looked pretty angry, and I was a bit hesitant to go in without someone else present, so I just told him I'd wait in the car until the lawyer arrived."

"You were afraid of violence?" Nikki asked.

"I just felt uneasy. I didn't think he would kill me in his house, since that would make him a prime suspect. But, as they say, discretion is the better part of valor, and I didn't think anything would transpire until his lawyer arrived anyway."

Archie asked, "Did you tell anyone you were going to his house?"

"No, I didn't think to."

"Why didn't you bring a lawyer?" Nikki asked.

"I didn't think I could arrange that on such short notice, and I didn't expect to close the deal that night in any case, without paperwork a lawyer could review. I certainly wasn't going to bring cash to close a deal."

"I see," Nikki said. "So what happened?"

"He said he would call the lawyer to see what delayed him, and went back in the house. I went back to my car and listened to a streaming radio business channel."

"Which one?" Archie inquired.

Michalopoulos looked puzzled at the seemingly irrelevant question. "I think it was the Economist channel," he said.

"Go on," Nikki said.

"I sat there for about 15 minutes, and then rang the doorbell again. When Hoskins opened the door, he said the attorney couldn't make it—a personal emergency, he said—and we'd have to do it some other time. I was angry and told him next time, he'd have to come to my office. I left."

"You never even went in the house?" Nikki asked.

"No," Michalopoulos said. He paused. "The news report said that he was dead under suspicious circumstances, but gave no details. What happened?"

"He was shot," Nikki said. "Do you own a gun?"

"No," Michalopoulos said. "And it's ridiculous to even consider me a suspect. Why would I kill him? What could I possibly gain? And, if I killed him, would I admit I was there last night?"

"You might if there was other evidence we could find that showed you were there," Archie said. "Hoskins' lawyer would know about the scheduled meeting. And we could possibly track your car. The car infotainment system you were using has a GPS and tracks your movements so it can answer questions like the nearest gas station or provide driving directions." He moved the smartwatch near his mouth. "Erasmus, where was George Michalopoulos last night about 9 PM?"

There was a pause. Erasmus said, "A car registered to George Michalopoulos arrived at 980 Moorpark Road at 9 PM and remained for 21 minutes." The address was Hoskins'.

Michalopoulos looked surprised. "Is that legal?" he said.

Archie responded, "I suspect it couldn't be used in court, but it makes my point."

Michalopoulos frowned. "Well, it simply validates my story."

"Only that you were there for twenty-one minutes," Archie said.

Michalopoulos said impatiently, "This is ridiculous! Why would I kill him?! And, certainly, if I even had a motive, why would I make myself such an obvious suspect?"

"That is puzzling to me as well," Archie said. Nikki looked annoyed at him for apparently agreeing with Michalopoulos. But he added, "Perhaps it was urgent because he had something on you he was going to reveal."

Michalopoulos took a deep breath. "And what would that be?"

"I'll try to find out," Archie said. "Erasmus will help. As you've seen, he can be quite informative," he continued, glancing at his smartwatch. "Anything you want to tell us now?"

"I don't have anything to hide. Hoskins hated me for my success in competing with him, nothing more. If he had anything to hurt me with, he would have used it long ago. You will just waste your time digging for some dirt."

"Well," Nikki smiled. "Digging does often result in dirt."

Michalopoulos looked angry. "Yes, and if you fabricate some lies on flimsy evidence, I'll sue. Hoskins set this up somehow. Are you sure it wasn't suicide, and him trying to get back at me in the process?"

Nikki said, "The evidence seems to rule out suicide."

"Why?" Michalopoulos asked.

"I can't go into details."

"Well," Michalopoulos retorted. "Since you obviously won't listen to reason, I won't talk further without my lawyer."

Nikki raised an eyebrow and looked at Archie as if Michalopoulos had declared himself guilty. The lawyer comment ended the conversation, and Nikki and Archie left.

Chapter 5

As they drove away, Nikki said, "I'm surprised he admitted he was there with Hoskins. Then again, he didn't have much choice if he believed Hoskins' lawyer would have been informed of the meeting, including the statement that Michalopoulos would be there. Rather than get caught in an incriminating lie if, for example, we could prove his car was there through surveillance video or other means, he would have to admit he was there."

"Did the video surveillance show anything?" Archie asked.

"Apparently, it was turned off. I guess Hoskins only turned on the security system when he left the house. Most people don't want constant video of themselves in the house. Ever since a hacker distributed video of a TV personality undressing, obtained using her own security cameras, some people have become paranoid about such things."

"But what about the outside surveillance? Did he leave that on?"

"No, that was also shut off, although it could be controlled separately," Nikki said, looking puzzled.

"That doesn't make sense," Archie said. "But he may have just shut everything off to avoid having to deal with complex controls. Today's digital devices let you have so many options, they sometimes become unusable."

"Also, if Michalopoulos is telling the truth, and the lawyer arrived after he left, the lawyer is a suspect," she said. "Can you arrange an interview with the lawyer?"

Archie said, "Erasmus, show me the info on John Taver." Erasmus displayed the previously collected information on Taver.

"Call him." Archie took his smartphone from his pocket. It was ringing the lawyer's office as he did.

A receptionist answered. "Taver and Schmidt law offices. How can I help you?"

"I'd like to speak to John Taver."

"Who's calling?"

"Archibald Teal. He doesn't know me, but I'm calling regarding one of his clients."

"OK. Please hold."

Taver came on the line. "John Taver, how can I help you?"

"Police business, Mr. Taver. Your client, Edward Hoskins, was found dead today, and we have a few questions."

"I heard, and he's no longer my client."

"Obviously," Archie said. "He's dead."

"I mean I ceased being his lawyer last week. He had outstanding legal bills and no prospect of paying them. I told him I could no longer represent him until back bills were paid."

"Weren't you going to his house last night?"

"Of course not. I haven't heard from him since I talked to him last week."

"We heard differently."

"Well, you heard wrong."

Nikki whispered, "Ask where he was last night."

"Where were you last night, Mr. Taver?"

"At home with my wife," he said. "And, since you seem to be treating me as a suspect, I won't answer any more questions without my attorney."

"Can we validate your presence with your wife?"

"No more questions for either of us without our lawyer."

Archie ended the call without a word.

Nikki said, "That's interesting. Suppose he's telling the truth. Then, no lawyer was ever going to show up. But, why would Michalopoulos lie?"

"It doesn't make sense he would lie about that, since believing the lawyer knew of the meeting would be the most likely reason he admitted being there. Otherwise, he wouldn't even be a suspect if we hadn't found the calendar entry on Hoskins' laptop."

"Then Hoskins was lying about the lawyer, presuming we accept the lawyer's story," Nikki said. "Why would he do that?"

"To get Michalopoulos to come over, perhaps. Otherwise, Michalopoulos might have been wary, if the two of them were going to be alone. Or the lawyer could have been lying, come over and killed Hoskins, knowing that Michalopoulos would become the prime suspect. We need to try to find out if the lawyer had any reason to want Hoskins dead."

Nikki smiled. "Perhaps he thought he could get his bills paid when the estate was liquidated."

Archie took her seriously. "If he was essentially bankrupt, the chances would be slim—too slim to justify the risk of murder."

"Yes, Archie," she said, still smiling. "Just in case, we should subpoena the lawyer's records to find the amount owed; but mostly to validate that he cancelled Hoskins as a client. I'll get that in process when we get back to the office, which is where I'm heading now, unless you want me to drop you off at home."

"The office is fine."

They stopped at a light.

"How was your date yesterday?" Archibald asked.

"My date? What makes you think I had a date yesterday?"

"You wore a dress to work."

23

"You noticed?"

"Of course. You have very nice legs."

"Archibald! I didn't think you noticed."

"Don't most men?"

Nicki hesitated. "Yes. Unfortunately, it seems the first thing most men notice about me is how I look. I thought you were above that."

Archibald thought back to when he first met Nicki. "I did notice you were beautiful when we first met. All I knew before we even talked was how you looked. But I also noticed you didn't seem to want to emphasize your asset."

Nicki wondered if she should react to the possible pun, but realized that Archibald didn't usually attempt jokes. "How is that?"

"You were wearing a loose blouse and slacks that looked like they'd been washed many times. And your hair was pulled back in a ponytail that suggested you didn't want to spend much time with it in the morning."

"Always logical. You're right. I've just found that men either assume an attractive woman will simply rely on beauty to get ahead or is simply too dumb to do otherwise. Or, even worse, that I'm just looking for a man to take care of me."

Archibald looked puzzled. "But it doesn't take long to find out you're smart and highly motivated. Don't men adjust their point of view when they get to know you?"

"I'm afraid they do, and then most feel challenged and disappear quickly. The more confident men tend to choose a woman with a less demanding job—or maybe one that seems more 'feminine' or less assertive."

She thought a moment. "Or maybe I fight any feelings of affection because I don't want to be dependent on someone else. That may give the impression to a man that I don't like him."

"What about your date?"

"I don't just wear a dress because I have a date. I sometimes dress up a bit because I have to interview a suspect that I think might be distracted by a little cleavage or legs, and let something slip."

"But you didn't interview anyone yesterday."

"OK. I had a date. I met a guy for drinks after work. A guy I met at a coffee shop over the weekend. He asked me out, and I decided to give it a try."

"So, did you have sex?"

"He bent me over the bar stool and took me right there. The bartender asked us to take it elsewhere…after we paid the bill."

"Didn't all the people in the bar make you uncomfortable?" Archibald responded, apparently unaware that she was being sarcastic.

She stopped at a light and looked at him, always amazed at his tendency to take everything seriously. "Well, my date had an overcoat that he put over us."

Archibald looked puzzled. "It's too warm for an overcoat."

"It was his 'sex-in-a-bar' overcoat."

There was a brief silence. Archibald suddenly got it. "You're kidding me, aren't you?"

Nikki gave him an unbelieving look.

"OK. Did you have sex with him?"

"Archibald, didn't your mother tell you that you shouldn't ask such questions?"

"I don't remember my mother mentioning anything about sex. Did you have sex with him?"

Nikki responded with silence.

Chapter 6

As they walked into the precinct, Nikki asked, "Should we try to get a warrant to search Michalopoulos' house?"

"Well, we have enough, with his admission of being at the scene of the killing at the right time. If he did it, we won't find a gun or bloody clothes. He's had enough time to make sure there is no evidence, but it's worth a try. Maybe during the search we'll find something that helps."

"I'll get that started," she said, as they reached her desk. Jim Adams, an officer at the next desk, commented, "Hot case, huh?"

"Yeah," Nikki said. "This one has already made the news."

"Erasmus gonna solve it, Archie?" Adams asked, smiling.

Archie said, "No, Nikki and I are going to solve it, if you don't bother us."

Adams looked annoyed and went back to studying a file on his desk. Nikki looked at Archie disapprovingly.

Archie didn't seem to notice. "The calendar entry said, 'Tell Michalopoulos what I've got on him,'" he said. "I'll get Erasmus started on collecting anything that could help us understand what Hoskins was referring to. If there is a dark secret, that could be the real motivation to Michalopoulos being willing to go alone at night to Hoskins' house. And a reason to murder him."

Archie said to his smartwatch, "Erasmus, deep background on Edward Hoskins. Focus on possible illegal activities."

"Archie," Nikki said. "Not out loud. I'm working."

Archie switched to his smartphone to type to Erasmus, touching the "silent" icon in the Erasmus app, notifying Erasmus to respond by text. He typed, "Look for illegal behavior by George Michalopoulos of Interactive Apps. Make it exhaustive." The last statement was an instruction to Erasmus to make the search in-depth, using all assets available to him, including the NSA connection. If there was any sign of illegal activity by Michalopoulos, it wouldn't be from easily accessible resources. Erasmus vibrated to indicate that he understood.

After some typing on her PC, Nikki said, "OK. The search warrant is in the works."

"One thing bothers me," Archie said.

"What's that?"

"Michalopoulos said suicide was a possibility. It apparently isn't, because no gun was found. Why didn't the killer leave the gun in Hoskins' hand to create doubt that it wasn't a murder?"

"I thought about that, too," Nikki said. "But the gun might have been one that could be traced to the killer."

"And why didn't the killer shoot Hoskins in a spot more certain to kill him?" Archie continued, revisiting a prior concern.

Nikki said, "Perhaps Hoskins tried to grab the gun, took a shot to the abdomen, and the killer panicked and ran."

"That's possible," Archie said. "In any case, the lack of a gun with death by gunshot makes it obviously not a suicide."

Chapter 7

When Archie arrived at the precinct the next day, Nikki said that the autopsy report was ready. "Let's hear it and see if we need to talk to the pathologist," she said.

Archie said, "Send it to Erasmus." Nikki did. When the phone beeped to acknowledge receipt, Archie said, "Erasmus, summarize autopsy report through the phone," placing his smartphone on the desk in speakerphone mode.

Erasmus replied. "Report received. The victim died from loss of blood from a single shot to the abdomen. The shot missed the spine, leaving the victim mobile other than the injury. Victim died about 10 PM the day before the body was discovered. There was a high level of painkiller found in his blood. After further examination, the pathologist found that he had an advanced case of pancreatic cancer, motivating the use of the painkiller. The disease appears to have progressed to the stage where he would have died in a few months. No further main findings."

Nikki said, "I guess the killer didn't know of Hoskins' condition."

"Or couldn't wait until he died," Archie countered. "Perhaps it was necessary to silence him quickly. That would be the case if Hoskins had something on Michalopoulos."

"We should check Hoskins' PC and any other digital storage more closely to see if something is there. And we should probably talk to our pathologist directly to see if he can provide anything further; but we can put that off until we know more."

They left for Hoskins' house. As they drove, Archie said suddenly, "Nikki, will you go out on a date with me?"

Nikki suspected this would eventually come up, since Archie had signaled his interest. She'd thought about how to respond. Archie was trim and had a strong, masculine face, and she admired his intelligence. But his lack of social skills made her feel that a long-term relationship might be difficult. She wondered if his interest in her was basically sexual, and whether he even understood the concept of love. On the surface, she was tough, but at a deeper level, she was increasingly looking for the warmth and companionship of a long-term relationship, what most people called "love."

She reviewed her thoughts about the matter while trying to decide how to respond to Archie's invitation. If a relationship developed, it might also be difficult to associate with others outside of work, since Archie's lack of understanding of social interaction could make it difficult to retain real friendships with others as a couple. She wasn't particularly social herself, but did have some long-term friendships with individuals and couples that she prized, even if she saw them infrequently. Of course, a date didn't necessarily imply a long-term relationship—or even sex—but it could complicate their productive professional partnership.

Archie repeated, as if she hadn't heard, "Will you go out on a date with me?"

Since subtlety wasn't Archie's strong suit, she decided to get to the point. "Archie, why do you want to go on a date with me?"

"I like being around you."

"Well, you're around me almost every day. Why a date?"

"Well, when I'm with you at work, we mostly talk about cases. When we go out on a date, we could talk about more personal things."

"We could simply talk about more personal things during work hours, when we are between cases or waiting for something we need to proceed. A 'date' implies an interest in more dates and perhaps a long-term relationship if things work out. Or, I guess it could just be an interest in having a short-term sexual connection. What are you implying by a 'date'?"

Archie looked confused. "When I go on a date, it's usually because I want to have sex with the woman. I try to impress her with my PhD and imply I'm good at sex."

Nikki smiled. "Impressive. How well does that work?"

"Not too well, but sometimes it works."

"I guess 'works' means you have sex."

"Yes. And sometimes they are willing to go out on a date again."

"More sex, I presume."

"Yes, but the ones that are willing to have more dates start to demand things of me that don't involve sex, like going to parties with them. I sometimes try to accommodate the ones that are most attractive, but I eventually drop the relationship if it starts getting to be demanding. Sometimes they drop it because they realize I'm mostly interested in sex with them and no more."

"Archie, I'm hesitant to get involved with a colleague to begin with, and your description of your relationships doesn't sound inviting at all."

Archie looked dismayed, an expression Nikki didn't remember seeing before. "You asked what dating was for me, and I was describing what it was with other women. You're different."

Nikki was surprised. "How am I different?"

"You're Nikki. I don't think of you the same way as other women."

Nikki had expected this conversation to end quickly with a "no" from her, but she was intrigued. "Explain."

"Well, I like to be with you even without sex. I like to talk to you. I like to look at you. I like the sound of your voice. I'm impressed with your drive and self-confidence. It's not something I've felt with other women, and I really don't know how to say it."

Nikki was taken aback. He could have been describing "love," but she suspected that was a feeling he didn't comprehend. She hesitated and Archie said, "I want to understand these feelings better. I'd like to have intercourse with you, but I'd like to go out with you even if that wasn't part of the date."

She suddenly realized that Archie was the only man in her life that truly intrigued her, and that she had been burying these feelings out of concern for the downside without considering the upside. "Archie, I'll go out on a date with you to talk more personally, but don't expect anything beyond that."

He looked relieved and excited at the same time. "How about going out to dinner Saturday? I'll get a recommendation from Erasmus for a good restaurant and pick you up at your apartment at seven. OK?" He rushed out the words as if she might change her mind.

She smiled. "It's a date. Tell Erasmus to pick a place that isn't too noisy so we can talk."

Archie suddenly seemed to be speechless. Nikki warned, "And let's not talk about dates in the office."

"OK," Archie said.

Chapter 8

On the way to Michalopoulos' house, with Nikki driving, Archie checked Erasmus' analysis of possible illegal activities by Michalopoulos. "Erasmus is still searching," Archie said. "So far, he indicates that the growth of Michalopoulos first company, the game company, is anomalous in that it was so fast and large compared to the uptake of new mobile games, despite being sold directly instead of through app stores. It's not unprecedented, but unusual, particularly for a game that isn't free. And Erasmus indicates that there wasn't as much social networking about the apps compared to other similar successes. Social discussion of successful games drives sales, but there was little of that with Michalopoulos' games. People simply bought the games. Erasmus classifies it as a statistical anomaly."

Nikki commented, "That sounds like something to dig into."

"Yes," Archie said. "Erasmus is going to go deeper using his full resources and try to see if he can understand more."

They had access to Hoskins' house as a crime scene. They first checked his PC, using the password they had discovered earlier. They took the most obvious route, simply searching the hard drive for any documents mentioning Michalopoulos or his company. Several documents of possible interest turned up, and Archie plugged his smartphone into the PC and said, "Erasmus, get a copy of the listed documents and summarize," highlighting the results of the search. "We'll look at them in detail later," he said to Nikki, "but let's get a feel for what we have."

Erasmus scanned the long list of documents the search had turned up. Archie's smartwatch vibrated after a few minutes, and Archie looked at the screen. "The summary is ready." He had Erasmus speak the summary on the smartphone's speakerphone. "One category of documents was not created by Hoskins," Erasmus said. "They are news items, press releases, and publicity or marketing documents that mention Michalopoulos or Interactive Apps, Incorporated. There are a number pre-dating Interactive Apps about Michalopoulos' prior career."

Archie paused Erasmus. "It sounds as if Hoskins was doing his own research. Erasmus, continue."

"There are a number of documents and e-mails that were created by Hoskins that mention Michalopoulos. Most of the earlier ones are business communications about the competition he presented. They appear to be normal business discussions about what Interactive Apps was doing and how to respond. I've prepared a list of the people, mostly in his company or public relations firm, that he corresponded with, along with their e-mail addresses and what I can find about where they are and what they are doing now."

"Erasmus," Archie interrupted. "Use this information to supplement your research about possible illegal activities by Michalopoulos. Check if any of these people connected to Hoskins are also connected to Michalopoulos."

He turned to Nikki. "Perhaps someone in Hoskins' firm was bribed by Michalopoulos to provide confidential information or technology."

"We should interview some of his employees and associates in any case," Nikki said.

Archie nodded in agreement. "Erasmus, continue."

"Some later documents note what I found earlier, that Michalopoulos' game company had an unusually fast start. Hoskins has numbers on game sales from public documents, but doesn't have any real statistical analysis. He simply notes that they seem suspicious. I see some efforts at further analysis, but they don't seem to have gone very far. I see e-mails where he inquired on fees for private investigators to dig deeper, but he doesn't seem to have retained an investigator. Most firms responded to his inquiries by saying they needed more information to give a quote, and just gave hourly rates and a retainer fee. They offered to meet with him to discuss the task in more detail."

Archie interrupted again. "Erasmus, what is the date of these e-mails to private investigators."

"March 8 through March 16," Erasmus said.

"That was after he was in financial trouble," Archie said to Nikki. "He probably decided he didn't have the money to hire investigators."

"Or the time," Nikki said. "He was dying."

Archie nodded. "Erasmus, continue."

"Some e-mails deal with the denial-of-service attacks and credit card thefts. He notes that Michalopoulos had a background working in security services before he launched the game company. Hoskins asked his IT department if they could trace the attacks to Michalopoulos. Responding e-mails indicate no success in doing so, noting the difficulty of tracing attacks of this sort in general. The highest scoring document on possible illegal activities by Michalopoulos is the last, written on April 10."

"That's the day before he was shot," Nikki said, raising her eyebrows.

Erasmus continued. "The document lists a number of illegal things that it claims Michalopoulos could have done, and claims that Hoskins has evidence of them. The document claims that game purchases in the game company were fraudulent, without specifying why, and that Michalopoulos was responsible for the hacking attacks on Involvement.com. This concludes the summary."

"Erasmus, show me the last document," Archie said, looking at his phone screen. The document appeared. "It's pretty short," Archie said. "Just more or less claiming what Erasmus said, with no indication of what the evidence is or its source."

"It could have been what Hoskins was going to show Michalopoulos, and demand something to not release the information."

"But that wouldn't have been very convincing without more details about what would be revealed," Archie said.

"But it provides a clear motive for Michalopoulos to kill him. Perhaps Hoskins gave enough details when they met to convince Michalopoulos he was a threat. Or at least bluffed convincingly. Hoskins was desperate for cash."

Archie said, "We'll have to look more carefully into this. Erasmus, please send all relevant documents from this PC to cloud storage."

They spent some time looking for possible paper documents in Hoskins' files. But, as one might expect in a digital age, there were few documents in the files, and none that appeared relevant. When they gave up on finding more, Archie asked Erasmus for a prioritized list of employees of Hoskins' firm that were addressees of Hoskins' e-mails about Michalopoulos.

Archie looked at the list. "It looks as if the IT manager, Jason Williamson, is the most relevant one to contact. Erasmus has provided Williamson's phone number and address."

"Williamson's contact information provided," Erasmus said, apparently responding to his name.

Nikki smiled. "Thanks, Erasmus," she said.

35

"You're welcome," Erasmus replied.

Nikki was amused that Erasmus had more manners than Archie usually did. "Let's call Williamson and see if we can talk to him today."

They did, and he said he was available. They drove to his office.

Chapter 9

Williamson had moved to another technology firm as IT manager with the demise of Involvement.com. He greeted them, expressing his horror at having heard his former boss was dead, possibly murdered. "He was a brilliant guy, and didn't deserve what happened to his company."

"So we understand," Nikki said. "Do you have any idea who might have wanted him dead?"

"Not really. He wasn't the kind of guy who created enemies, even in business. The only person he was really angry with was George Michalopoulos of Interactive Apps, the company that competed in an area he pioneered. Even there, he didn't attack Michalopoulos personally, but tried to compete fairly in the marketplace. Privately, he suspected Michalopoulos was competing unfairly, even illegally. But, don't quote me on that."

"Can you elaborate?" Nikki asked.

"Well, my responsibility is managing computer operations. I had to recover from denial-of-service attacks that made our service largely unusable for a period of time, as well as the later hacking of credit card information. Edward suspected that somehow Michalopoulos was behind those events, and asked me to prove it. The only real evidence he suggested was Michalopoulos' background in security. He worked for a company researching hackers and creating security solutions to defend big companies."

He continued, "I didn't really think that Michalopoulos would risk doing something illegal, and these things are difficult to trace, as many companies larger than us—including the US government—have found. So I told him there was essentially no chance of tracing the activities to Michalopoulos, and I didn't have the bandwidth to try to both avoid a repeat of the problems and also be an investigator."

Nikki asked, "So you didn't find anything connecting the intrusions to Michalopoulos?"

"No. If I'd found anything I could have followed up with any prospect of success, I would have. Whoever attacked the company hurt my reputation as well as the company."

Archie asked, "How hard was it to steal the credit card data? Did you have strong security measures?"

"Don't quote me on this," Williamson replied, "but Hoskins didn't make security a priority, and didn't let us spend much in that area. So we had only some basic security measures. I suspect they wouldn't have been a huge challenge to a skilled hacker. To his credit, Edward didn't blame me for the intrusions—he knew I had recommended we spend more on security."

"Did you have any direct connections to Michalopoulos?" Archie asked.

Williamson looked annoyed. "Are you asking if he was a friend? I would have made a bunch from Involvement.com stock if we went public as planned, and he destroyed that opportunity, as well as my job. My job didn't allow much involvement with him, even if he'd tried to connect. I'd met him a few times at industry events and social occasions, but it didn't go beyond an uncomfortable handshake."

Nikki changed the subject. "Is there anything more you can say about Hoskins' attitude toward Michalopoulos?"

"Well, in informal conversations, he told me he thought there was something fishy about the game company that was Michalopoulos original success. His reason for thinking so seemed pretty vague."

They continued with a few more questions that were mostly versions of the same questions. Nothing useful surfaced.

Chapter 10

Archie arrived to pick Nikki up for their date at exactly the scheduled time. Archie hadn't told her what restaurant Erasmus had chosen, so she had agonized briefly over whether dressy or casual attire was appropriate. She decided that if she was going to give a relationship with Archie a chance, she should optimize it and wear something that was a great deal more feminine than office attire. She chose a dress that showed both legs and cleavage. When she opened her apartment door to Archie's ring, the look on his face confirmed her choice.

"Hi," he gulped, looking at all of her, not just her face. "You look different."

She smiled. "Is that a compliment or a criticism of my work clothes?"

"I like both, but these clothes are more sexy."

She was glad she dressed up, since Archie was wearing a sports jacket. He looked very handsome, she thought. "And you look pretty good yourself," she said. He looked pleased.

As they walked to the car, she asked, "So, are we going out for hamburgers?"

Archie said, "Is that what you want? Erasmus picked an Italian restaurant that Yelp rated highly."

Nikki touched his arm reassuringly. He seemed to tremble. "I was just joking."

As they drove to the restaurant, Archie seemed to be at a loss for words. "What do you usually talk about when you go out on a first date?" she asked, hoping to start a conversation.

"Well, I've usually told them before the date what I do, so they usually ask me about my job as a detective.

Usually, I tell them about a case and how we solved it."

Nikki raised an eyebrow. "We? You don't actually talk about me, I hope."

"Well, I don't tell them how beautiful you are, just that I work with you."

"I appreciate the compliment, but doesn't explaining a case take a lot of time?"

Archie thought a moment. "Well, yes, but then I don't run out of things to say."

"Don't you want to hear something about your date? Don't you ask about them?"

Archie looked taken aback. "I guess I should."

"You're charming, Archie," she smiled. "Don't they get annoyed if you don't give them a chance to talk?"

Archie looked as if he had just heard a deep revelation. "They do get annoyed sometimes, and I guess that must be the reason why."

Nikki smiled. "I guess if this date doesn't work out, you've learned something that will help with other dates."

Archie looked at her longingly. "I hope this date works out."

Nikki was a bit surprised by Archie's sincerity. She hoped it wasn't just a sexual interest.

"Well," she said. "I guess you don't have to tell me what you do."

Archie, apparently trying to take her advice, said, "Tell me about you."

"Archie, you know a lot about me. I'm not sure what to say."

"Tell me something I don't know."

Nikki thought. "Well, you've heard that I grew up in a small town in Texas, went to college in LA, and stayed here. I've told you I liked mystery novels and that led me to apply for a job with the police and worked to become a detective. My major was sociology, and there weren't too many jobs in that field without an advanced degree."

"Well, tell me more about growing up in a small town."

"We only had one high school, but I guess going to high school is the same everywhere. Our teachers were generally very good, mostly women. Perhaps that was because a number of wives of men working in local oil production were well educated, and teaching was one of the professions in a small town where they could use their education."

"Did you date a lot?" Archie asked.

"Archie, you always seem to return to my relationships with men. It was high school, and of course I had dates. A lot of girls ended up getting married to high-school sweethearts—first love and all that, I guess—and staying in town. I avoided getting too involved with any one person. Partially, that was because none of them really intrigued me, but probably mostly because I wanted to go to college and experience more than a small town."

"What about college?" Archie said.

Nikki laughed. "Archie, you've learned your lesson too well. We should have a conversation, not a series of speeches."

Archie thought for a moment. "What do you think of the president's speech today?"

Nikki managed not to laugh at the obvious attempt to start an interactive conversation. "I guess we could talk about world affairs, but I didn't mean to just make conversation to make conversation. What interests you that might interest me?"

He gave the obvious answer. "Our current case."

Nikki nodded. "Well, I guess we shouldn't talk about work on a date, but, honestly, it's been on my mind, too. Michalopoulos is the most obvious suspect, of course, but something doesn't feel right."

"I feel uncomfortable as well," Archie said. "It seems too open and shut, and he's too bright to have made himself such an obvious suspect. And, if he was guilty, he wouldn't have said anything to us at all without a lawyer."

"His story was almost too strange, claiming he didn't even go inside the house," Nikki added. "If he were guilty, I suspect he would have said he went in the house, in case we found his DNA on something."

She paused. "On the other hand, perhaps the crime wasn't premeditated. He might have been afraid of Hoskins, and brought a gun just in case Hoskins was determined to have revenge, particularly if Michalopoulos knew he was dying. Michalopoulos might have just taken out the gun in fear of a Hoskins' threat, and shot him by accident when Hoskins tried to grab the gun, as I suggested before."

"But," Archie said, "if that were the case, why not admit that Hoskins attacked him and he shot in self-defense or by accident? That would be pretty credible, since Hoskins obviously had a grudge. He could have put a knife in Hoskins' hand, for example, and claimed he was attacked with it."

"There are too many holes, although there certainly is enough evidence to arrest him, if it would serve any purpose."

"He would just post bail," Archie said. "We're better off if he thinks we're looking elsewhere. He might give us something if he thinks it will throw us off the trail."

They arrived at the restaurant, interrupting the conversation. They were escorted to their table. Archie asked, "I usually order wine. Would you like something else?"

"No," Nikki said. "I like wine."

"What kind?" Archie said.

"Well, I'll have fish, I think, so white wine, maybe Chardonnay."

"I'll order a bottle," Archie said, looking at the wine menu. He raised his watch and said, "Erasmus, which is best, Red Creek Chardonnay or Chateau Lehman?"

Nikki couldn't resist a smile. Archie was Archie.

Erasmus provided recommendations. Archie said, "Of the two most expensive Chardonnays on the menu, Red Creek is rated highest."

"That sounds good," Nikki said. She didn't coyly protest that he shouldn't spend too much; she knew he had made a lot of money after leaving the government as a consultant on the hit spy movie about cybersecurity. He still consulted for companies on that subject at an outrageous hourly rate. He took only a token consulting fee from the police department, indicating he considered detective work a hobby.

While waiting for the wine, they studied the menu, and ordered when the waiter brought the wine.

"So," Nikki said, reopening the conversation. "Who did it, if not Michalopoulos?"

Archie said, "The lawyer is the only one that evidence suggests might have been there. Oh, and I forgot to tell you, Erasmus supports the fact that Hoskins was no longer a client. He hacked the customer accounting records at Taver's firm—they weren't as well protected as the actual legal files—and found unpaid bills for Hoskins and a notation from two weeks ago that he was a 'discontinued' client."

"Well, he said he was home and his wife could vouch for him, which I guess she would in any case. But we certainly don't have any real evidence of his being at Hoskins' house, or a motive."

The waiter served their salads, and Nikki said, "In any case, as much as this case intrigues me, we said we would use a date to talk more personally."

"I think I love you," Archie said.

"Well, you certainly don't mince words," Nikki said, surprised by his abrupt statement, but secretly pleased. "I'm flattered, but what do you mean by that?"

"I'm not sure," Archie said. "I've never felt this way. I just can't get enough of you somehow."

Nikki was speechless, not sure how to react. Archie added, "I don't ever want to not be around you." He looked flustered. "That's a double negative. I want to be around you always."

"Archie, that's a strong statement. I guess that is one way to express love." She felt that his declaration demanded a statement from her about her feelings.

"Archie, I am attracted to you, both because I enjoy working with you, because of your intelligence, and you are a handsome man. But I wouldn't call it 'love' at this point. I'm a bit uncomfortable with taking our relationship in that direction."

"Why?" Archie asked.

"Archie, you know you have trouble dealing with emotions and interacting with people at more than a superficial level. If we had a long-term relationship, I'm afraid we'd be isolated, that we wouldn't have friends as a couple. I even wonder if your feelings of love are driven more by unrequited sexual desire than what I would call 'love,' since, as you say, you're not sure what those feelings are."

Archie looked dismayed. "I understand what you're saying," he said after a pause. "I've always had trouble understanding how to interact with people in a way that pleases them. I haven't needed social contact to be happy. I've always had intellectual interests that were my major priority and source of satisfaction. So I guess

45

I've never been motivated to try to overcome my social limitations. I'll try to do better."

Nikki found that she wanted to accept that he could become more social. And, if she was honest, she was a bit of a loner herself. Perhaps they were a better match than she let herself admit. And she even found herself wondering what sex with him would be like. But she told herself to move slowly.

"Archie, I'm willing to continue to explore a closer relationship, but I don't want to move too fast."

Archie appeared relieved. "That's all I ask," he said.

They did manage to talk casually for the rest of the dinner, discussing what each liked to do outside of work. When Archie took her home, she didn't invite him in. She wasn't quite ready for that. Archie didn't attempt a kiss, and she didn't initiate one. But she did agree to another date in a few days.

Chapter 11

Archie wasn't ready to sleep when he got home. He was too excited. Nikki was willing to continue a relationship outside of work. The date had been different from any other date he'd had. On those dates, he felt he was working, mostly with the objective of getting the woman to have sex with him. With Nikki, as much as he longed to hold her close, he enjoyed the date beyond anticipation of what might come next. Since he knew that he would see her again, at least at work, there was less pressure. And he didn't have to try to impress her; she was already aware of his accomplishments and abilities.

He thought about her concerns over his social skills. He knew he lacked in that area, but it hadn't been an important issue for him. Now it was, if it was a hurdle to a closer relationship with her. He turned to his usual source for information.

"Erasmus, can you teach me social skills?"

"I can summarize advice I find on the Web. Do you want to know how to make people you meet like you?"

"Yes."

"Well, the most common advice is to ask them about themselves. People like to talk about themselves."

"So, just let them talk?"

"No, other advice is to react warmly, paying attention, and asking questions that show you are listening and interested. You should react appropriately as well, looking at them as they speak, smiling if the content is funny, or frowning if it reflects some stress in their lives."

"Listen and react appropriately," Archie repeated, as if studying a lesson. "Erasmus, continue."

"When asked a question, you should respond warmly and either address the question, or, if it isn't something you want to address, find a way to politely change the subject. But keep your answers short to give them a chance to talk or ask another question."

Erasmus continued summarizing advice that was common across a number of high-ranked websites covering personal relations. "And when you meet someone, smile and look at them warmly, say a greeting such as 'Nice to meet you,' or, 'How are you?' If you are asked, 'How are you?' initially or in return, it is appropriate to say something simple, such as 'Fine, thanks.' Generally, at the point of meeting someone, they really don't want details."

"How are you? Fine, thanks," Archie repeated. He realized that what he considered meaningless clichés that he had avoided, such as 'Hello,' 'please,' and 'thank you', were not meaningless to others. They were a signal of respect for and recognition of the other person. Once he intellectualized the concept, he could understand it and apply it.

Erasmus went through a number of topics, including more on interacting with others, overcoming discomfort with social situations, and expanding one's social circle. Archie told Erasmus to stop when he thought he had as much as he could absorb in one sitting.

Chapter 12

The next morning, he pondered how he could show Nikki that he could be more social, and apply what he had learned. He could try in the police station with witnesses or suspects in her presence, but making friends with those individuals wasn't always appropriate. He needed a way to practice, and to show Nikki they could have a social life.

The closest thing to a friend he had at the Agency was Fred Norman, an analyst like himself that he worked with. Fred and he were similar in terms of intelligence and technical interests, but Fred was more social. He got married while they were working together, and he and his wife, Lizzie, had had Archie and a couple of other Agency friends over for dinner. Lizzie was smart, and everyone seemed to like her.

He didn't think to reciprocate the dinner after being at their place, a mistake according to Erasmus' lessons. He just assumed, since he was single, that it wasn't necessary.

He quickly dialed the mobile number that he had for Fred, intending to leave a message if Fred wasn't available. But "Fred here," was a quick response.

"Hi, Fred. It's Archie Teal."

Fred sounded legitimately enthusiastic. "Archie! Great to hear from you. How are you doing?"

"I'm doing fine," Archie said, remembering his lesson. "How are you…and Lizzie?" he thought to add.

"Both doing well, thanks," Fred said. "What's up?"

"Can you talk?" Archie asked, knowing that the Agency frowned on personal calls at work.

"Sure. I'm driving to work."

"I've been meaning to call you," he said, not entirely honestly, but realizing that Fred might have been disappointed that he didn't keep in touch. He was learning to put himself in the other person's head, he hoped. "I'd like to get together with you and Lizzie and introduce you to Nikki, my work partner in the police department and friend. Perhaps we can all meet for dinner, my treat."

"That would be great, Archie. Lizzie recently asked what you've been doing since you left the Agency to consult on that film. You'll have to bring us up to date."

Archie remembered his lesson. "And I've been wondering what's up with you. We'll have to have an updating session."

"So is this Nikki something serious?" he asked.

"I hope so," Archie said. "I work with her every day, but only recently went out on a date with her."

"What do you two do?'

"She's a police detective, and I help her solve crimes."

"Wow! I guess we were detectives too, but mostly trying to prevent crimes."

"That's an interesting way of looking at it," Archie replied.

"I'm almost at work," Fred said. "When would you like to get together?"

"I'm having dinner with Nikki Saturday. Would you and Lizzie like to join us?"

"I think that works. I'll have to double check with Lizzie. I'll call you back at this number tonight if that works."

"Great, Fred. I hope it works out."

"If not Saturday, we'll find another time. I'd love to hear more about what you're doing."

"Thanks, Fred. Good-bye."

Archie was elated when he hung up. He had even remembered to say good-bye. He had always been a good student.

Chapter 13

The next day at the office, Archie told Nikki that Fred and Lizzie might join them for dinner. She was surprised, and impressed that Archie was trying to address her concerns. He hadn't even mentioned Fred previously. "That's terrific, Archie. I'd love to meet them."

Archie turned to the case. He indicated that Erasmus had a preliminary report on possible illegal activities by Michalopoulos. "Erasmus first looked at his game company, his company after the security consulting job," Archie summarized for Nikki. "Erasmus found an interesting correlation using all his resources. The names of credit card purchasers of his games correlate closely with customers of the companies he helped with the security of their systems."

"Erasmus was able to get credit card numbers?"

"He didn't have to go that far. The card numbers were pretty heavily encrypted, but names weren't. Companies want customer service representatives to have access to which customers had which products or services, and the software supporting customer service agents isn't as well protected as the credit card files. So Erasmus was able to get names of customers that were in the database while Michalopoulos had access to the company databases as part of his job. He similarly was able to get customers that bought the games initially, the big spurt of business that called attention to the game company. The two match to a large degree, with about 90% certainty it isn't an accident."

"I'm not sure what that means," Nikki said.

"Well, Erasmus can't easily get credit card numbers at the companies, but Michalopoulos could have gotten access as part of his job to help the company protect that data. Even if Michalopoulos wasn't given direct access to the numbers, he was working behind their security firewall, so hacking them would have been fairly easy. So he could have stolen credit card numbers from many companies. And he could have used those numbers to charge game purchases to credit card holders that didn't buy the game. He waited long enough so that the connection to his security job wouldn't be a red flag if someone got suspicious."

"But wouldn't the cardholders complain and the fraud become obvious to credit card companies?"

"Well, if you see a charge of $4.99 on your credit card statement that you don't recognize, will you take the time to challenge it, or just assume it was a movie rental, song purchase, or something else you don't recognize? The charge was processed through a credit card processing service, so Michalopoulos' company name didn't show up, and the card processing service had some vague initials."

"But surely there were some challenges to the charges."

"And when the credit card company reversed the payments, Interactive Apps didn't challenge the reversal. Erasmus found that the company was challenged by one of the credit card companies, but apparently just claimed that people forgot they bought the game and they didn't think it worthwhile to pursue the payments if challenged. The amounts were small enough that the credit card company didn't pursue it."

Nikki thought a moment. "So he made his first fortune through fraud."

"Apparently."

"Can we prove it?"

"Erasmus' methods wouldn't hold up in court. But, if we tell credit card companies our suspicions, they might dig deeper. And the credit card company that found suspicious behavior and inquired would probably have a record that the case was only dropped because no more such charges came through and the amounts were too small. Too many coincidences of complaints beyond the statistical norm might allow them, with a court order, to provide incriminating details. That should be enough to get a court order to examine Interactive Apps' records and, with some luck, perhaps find the original databases, or match enough of them to companies where Michalopoulos had access, to make the evidence overwhelming."

Nikki said, "So we have evidence of motivation for murder if Hoskins had evidence of this."

Archie looked puzzled. "If Hoskins had such evidence, why didn't we find something more explicit on his PC? Nothing that explicit was mentioned when we talked to Williamson, his IT manager."

"He may simply have bluffed about having it, if he guessed."

Archie nodded. "Well, if we can't prove murder, we may at least have Michalopoulos for fraud. And, fortunately, we won't have to pursue this if we can get the FBI to do it. They have the authority and resources to do so."

"Will they believe us if we don't say why we suspect it?"

Archie smiled. "Well, I have a few contacts in their digital fraud unit from my past job. If I say I'm pretty sure based on looking at some statistics, without specifying the details, I have the credibility to motivate them to do their own investigation. I'll call one of my contacts later."

"Unfortunately, having a motive is supportive of his murdering Hoskins, but all our evidence is largely circumstantial. I'd like to have some physical evidence or something stronger before we arrest him. And we don't even have evidence of motive we can talk about until the FBI comes through, which could be a long while."

"Well," Archie said, "we might be lucky and find something when we search his house. And we can try to see if he was behind the denial-of-service attacks and credit card theft that were the nails in Involvement.com's coffin."

Nikki sighed. "And perhaps Hoskins' coffin as well."

"I'll put Erasmus to work more deeply on the hacking attacks," Archie said.

Chapter 14

They got the search warrant for Michalopoulos' house the next day. When they arrived with a couple of other policemen, Michalopoulos was there, looking annoyed and worried. While the other cops looked for guns—Michalopoulos claimed he didn't have one—Nikki and Archie went directly to Michalopoulos' PC. He had been using it, and hadn't turned it off when he went to the door, so they were lucky and didn't have to try to figure out a password or how to get through other security measures.

Michalopoulos stormed into the room. "You can't look at my PC!" he yelled.

"The search warrant covers your PC and any digital devices, including storage devices," Nikki said calmly.

Archie was plugging his phone in through a PC port. "Erasmus, search for and retain anything associated with Hoskins, Involvement.com, or any previous business files. Include any accounting files or other data files that might be relevant." He didn't explicitly tell Erasmus in front of Michalopoulos to search for passwords for any external storage sites Michalopoulos might have used for backup, but Erasmus would understand to recover any such information. Erasmus had been instructed that "other data files that might be relevant" was essentially all the information on the PC in case something turned out to be more relevant than an initial examination indicated.

Meanwhile, Nikki and Archie looked through the desk for any memory sticks or other digital storage devices. They did find a key that fit a fireproof file cabinet in the corner. "Most people would put something secret in the back folder of a file drawer,"

Nikki said, remembering a habit she had before realizing it was an obvious ploy to hide something. They did find a memory stick in an unmarked envelope in the last hanging file of the bottom drawer, the first place they looked.

"Always look first in the last place you would look," Nikki said. Michalopoulos was watching, and Nikki thought he looked upset.

They inserted it in the PC. The data was unreadable, apparently encrypted. "I'll take it home and see what I can do," Archie said. "If it's mild encryption, Erasmus may be able to break it in a day or two."

"A day or two?" Nikki said. "Isn't that slow for Erasmus?"

"It takes a lot of trial and error," Archie said. "He'll borrow some computing resources in the cloud, but it will take time."

The search didn't produce anything else of value. They left, with Michalopoulos slamming the door behind them.

Chapter 15

The next morning, while waiting for Erasmus to analyze the material from the Michalopoulos' search and come up with anything linking Michalopoulos to the hacking attacks on Involvement.com, they spent some time individually examining what evidence they had and thinking about the next steps. In the afternoon, they discussed their thoughts and concluded the best track was to see what Erasmus came up with.

"Erasmus, please give a status report on your investigations," Archie asked.

Erasmus was quiet for a moment. He said, "I don't understand 'investigations.'"

"That's strange," Archie said. "He always understands that to mean any pending research that hasn't been delivered or terminated."

"Erasmus," Archie said, looking alarmed. "What time is it?"

Erasmus was unresponsive for what seemed like a long time. "I will investigate," he said.

"Something's wrong." Archie looked alarmed. He took out his phone and started tapping on it, using the browser to access his private server. He studied the screen, reading and tapping. Nikki knew the best thing she could do was keep quiet and let him concentrate.

After some hectic activity, Archie said, "Someone is hacking Erasmus. He's using most of the server computing capabilities to block the attack and can't deal with our requests."

"Can you do anything?" Nikki looked worried. "Can't you cut off access to the server?"

"That's what Erasmus is trying to do, but whoever is doing this is apparently using sophisticated software beyond what we've seen before."

She had never seen Archie so rattled. In addition to the threat of the intrusion to their investigation, Nikki knew Erasmus was as close to a friend as Archie had, and it was as if his friend was being attacked in front of him.

"Archie, this must be Michalopoulos. It's too much of a coincidence that it happened the day after we got his files. Take a deep breath and think."

Archie stopped typing for a second and closed his eyes. "Oh," he said. "Maybe Erasmus saved some data on previous hacking by Michalopoulos in the cloud as part of my earlier inquiry." He began typing and reading again.

"I see it," Archie said. "Erasmus, use X2 defense modified with passcode al34d5uer."

Erasmus didn't immediately respond, then said, "Launching defense."

After a pause, Archie said, "Erasmus, report status."

Erasmus replied, "Attack slowed, but continues. High level of denial-of-service probes delaying my defense."

Archie thought a minute, and began typing. Then paused, "I rented additional servers and made them available to Erasmus," he explained.

"I didn't understand," Erasmus said, apparently thinking he had been addressed.

"Erasmus, report status."

"Closing outside access." A pause. "Access to outside attack closed. Cannot currently access outside resources. Attack continuing, but blocked currently."

Archie relaxed. "He's safe for a while unless the attacker tries a different attack, but I have to get back to the lab and repurpose some servers to give Erasmus more resources. I can't count on the outside servers not being attacked, since they aren't behind my firewall."

"Did he lose any information?" Nikki asked.

"I'll have to check, but it seems like he defended the data. He would have reported a data loss."

"I'll drive you home," Nikki said, "so you can work while I'm driving." Archie said nothing, but they ran to Nikki's car.

Chapter 16

Archie did indeed work intently while Nikki drove. "It's definitely Michalopoulos," he said, without taking his eyes off his phone's screen. "The attack tool matches a tool that Erasmus found earlier in a backup file Michalopoulos stored in the cloud. Because Erasmus downloaded the file to our cloud server, I could see it and realized that it probably provided a way to get behind our defenses if activated. Michalopoulos must have planted a virus we haven't seen before on his PC that would infect any device attached to it. That's how he got to Erasmus. He then penetrated our firewall from inside rather than outside. I'll have to make some changes so this can't happen again."

"So what are you going to do when we get there?" Nikki asked.

"Disconnect my home server physically from the Internet, get rid of the virus, add server capability to Erasmus so he has more computing power to fight off a hacking attack at the same time a denial-of-service attack is happening, change the software to prevent the specific virus and variations, and create a firewall that resists attacks from inside."

"That sounds like a lot to do," Nikki said.

"It might take me all night," Archie said. "I should have thought about this before."

"Could Erasmus have been destroyed?" Nikki said.

"I do have backups of his basic functionality, but recent data, including that from Michalopoulos, could have been destroyed if we hadn't noticed what was happening and interfered." Archie looked angry, an emotion she didn't remember seeing in him before. "We've got to put Michalopoulos in jail," he said.

"Isn't this enough to at least arrest him for trying to destroy evidence or more?"

"I'm not sure," Archie said. "It's very difficult to prove the source of a cyberattack if the attacker is sophisticated. And this is a very sophisticated attack. But there is obviously something he is trying to hide in the data we collected, or this wouldn't be necessary."

They arrived at the house, and Archie bounded from the car, unlocked his front door, and ran in. Nikki followed, well behind Archie.

As she went through the open front door, a dark figure wearing a ski mask ran into her, apparently attempting to run from the house and not expecting someone to be following Archie. She grabbed the man's jacket as he tried to run past her. He swung something at her head. She instinctively ducked, with the object barely missing, and dove for the person's legs, with both of them falling to the floor. "Archie, call 9-1-1!" she yelled.

She rolled away as the man swung the object at her again. The man jumped up and dashed for the door as Archie ran into the room. Nikki was still on the floor and reached for her gun. But it was strapped in with the safety on, since she didn't expect to be using it. The person was out the door before she could get it out. She sprang to her feet to chase the intruder, but Archie jumped in front of her and grabbed her arms. "Let him go," Archie said. "We don't know if he has a gun."

Nikki, frustrated, tried to get Archie to let go of her, but he was stronger than she anticipated. She finally gave up and said, "Did you call 9-1-1?"

"Not yet," Archie said, and took his phone from his pocket. They heard the squeal of car tires, presumably the intruder driving off.

"I'll report it," she said. "I'll get them to look for a vehicle speeding from this address." She made the call, and it wasn't too long before they heard the sounds of sirens.

"Wow," Nikki said. "What's going on today!?"

Archie acted more calm than he felt. "I suspect it was a continuation of Michalopoulos' attempts to destroy the data we collected. When I went into my study, I saw the window broken and open."

"So that was Michalopoulos?"

Archie shrugged. "Probably, since he didn't have a lot of time to draft someone to do it for him and explain how to destroy the data. He was wearing something over his face, so I can't be sure, but he was the same size as Michalopoulos."

Nikki suddenly felt a surge of panic. "Did he get the data?"

"No, my computer room is protected with a heavy door with a digital lock that requires my fingerprint." Archie said. "He didn't have time to get through that, although there are signs he tried to break it down."

Nikki noticed something on the floor. "He probably used that to try," she said, pointing to a small crowbar. "I suspect that was the weapon he tried to use on me."

Archie was startled, not having seen the original attack. "Are you all right?"

"Yes, I avoided the attack." Archie started to pick up the crowbar.

"Don't touch it!" Nikki warned. "It might have fingerprints or DNA. Wait for the crime scene documentation." As she finished, two policemen pushed through the open door. They recognized Nikki and, after ascertaining there were no injuries, began the job of documenting the attempted robbery and assault.

Nikki thought of something. She looked at her hand. There were a few threads of fabric, probably from the intruder's heavy jacket. "Get me a plastic bag," she said. Archie did, and she carefully brushed the few threads into the bag.

The police didn't locate the vehicle, since they had no description of it and it had apparently slowed down so that it wasn't obvious. The area had a relatively large amount of traffic, and many routes out, so setting up a perimeter wasn't practical; in any case, it was too late. Archie didn't have video surveillance at his house, but the police were going to check to see if there was anything in the neighborhood that might have caught the vehicle fleeing.

Archie did have an alarm system, but he seldom used it unless he was going to be away from the house overnight. He resolved to use it consistently whenever he left the house.

Archie had the police help him move a file cabinet in front of the broken window where the intruder had entered, resolving to call a repair service in the morning. He set about boosting Erasmus' computing power and security, and Nikki went home with a police escort that checked her house before she entered. She didn't see what Michalopoulos would gain by harming her, since the data was the incriminating evidence. But she admitted to herself that she wasn't as calm as she tried to appear.

Chapter 17

Archie didn't come into the office the next day, busy with getting his window repaired and napping after having worked most of the night. Nikki came in late and prepared her report. She left a bit early, since that evening was the night she was having dinner with Archie and his friend from the Agency. Archie and Nikki had discussed cancelling the date, but realized that it would be a welcome distraction from the drama of the previous day.

Archie in turn spent some time reviewing what Erasmus had taught him about being more sociable. He also took another lesson from Erasmus. Some of the advice was to bolster one's self-image, directed at individuals with little confidence. Archie didn't have that problem, just a lack of motivation to be social. Nikki had given him that motivation.

He admitted to himself that he felt satisfaction being reconnected with Fred Norman, and hoped the dinner would go well tonight; he resolved to maintain that connection. He thought a bit about how he should act with Fred and Lizzie, so that he could practice better social skills. Erasmus said that one should have "welcoming body language" when greeting or meeting someone, and described what was appropriate in different situations. Erasmus warned about over-doing being attentive or complimentary; he said to avoid the interaction becoming artificial and not natural. Humor lightened the conversation, if it wasn't too artificial; for example, telling long jokes not related to the conversation was too forced. Erasmus gave a few examples of inserting humor into a conversation. Like most things in his life, Archie was a good student when motivated. He thought he absorbed the lessons. The hard part would be internalizing them so they didn't come across as lessons he had learned.

Archie picked up Nikki. He remarked that she was even more beautiful than usual in tonight's evening attire. She quizzed him about the state of Erasmus and his house on the way to the restaurant, and he assured her that all was repaired; Erasmus' defenses were strengthened, and Erasmus was back to analyzing data. "He should be able to move faster with his increased computing resources," Archie indicated.

Fred and Lizzie arrived as they were waiting to be seated at the restaurant. Archie greeted Fred warmly with a firm handshake, and gave Lizzie a hug. "It's been a long time, Lizzie, but you are as beautiful as ever." He wasn't exaggerating; she was an attractive woman and, like Nikki, dressed to be noticed.

Fred said, "I see you're as perceptive as ever, Archie, and I must say that this lady with you is equally beautiful."

"This is Nikki, my friend and co-worker," he said. "Nikki, Fred and Lizzie."

They were shown to the table. "So, Archie. It's great to see you again," Fred said as they sat. "And this is the first time you've ever introduced me to a female friend."

Nikki said, "And this is the first time he's introduced me to friends outside of work."

Lizzie said, "It is indeed a pleasure to meet you. We haven't seen Archie in a long time, and it was a special surprise to hear from him."

Archie said, "Nikki and I work together, so we see each other almost every workday, but we've just begun dating." He didn't want Fred and Lizzie to assume too much.

"Well, thanks for including us on your date," Fred said.

The conversation ranged widely during dinner, from the menu to catching up with what all had been doing. Archie and Nikki stayed away from discussion of the current investigation. Archie was conscious of trying to practice his social lessons, but, as the dinner went on, he relaxed and found that the conversation wasn't a challenge. Fred and Lizzie understood him, and didn't react to the few times he felt he had said something perhaps a bit too nerdy. After all, Fred was a valid member of the nerd club himself. They left the restaurant promising to get together again soon.

As Archie drove Nikki home, she realized the warmth of the evening had largely erased the trauma of the previous day. She also was amazed by the change in Archie, and his ability to relate to his friends. It was at times obvious to her that he was working at it, but the fact that he was working at it endeared him to her.

Again, she just said goodnight at the door, wanting to continue to go slow. Archie left and got in his car. Before even starting the engine, he asked, "Erasmus, what is a romantic event or place for a date?"

Erasmus replied, "One suggestion I see on social networks is the Getty Museum just before sunset. Look at the view of LA, watch the sunset, take a look at the exhibits, and have dinner at the restaurant there."

Archie said, "Erasmus, call Nikki." Nikki answered, "Hi, Archie. It's been a long time."

"Not that long," Archie said, apparently missing the joke. "How about going to the Getty Saturday about five o'clock for the exhibits and an early dinner?"

"I'd love to, Archie."

"It's a date, and, if you can't wait to see me, I'll be at work tomorrow."

Nikki smiled. Archie was developing a sense of humor. "Tomorrow," she said, resisting an impulse to say, "How about now?"

Chapter 18

The next day, they reviewed evidence from the intrusion at Archie's house. They put a rush on the crowbar, but the attacker apparently was careful enough to use gloves and wipe the crowbar clean before he came to the house. The fibers Nikki grabbed might be useful later if they found a jacket belonging to Michalopoulos that matched them, but provided no immediate connection. The technical team was looking for video in the area that might show Michalopoulos' car, but hadn't yet found anything.

Nikki and Archie reviewed where they stood overall with the investigation, trying to determine the next steps. "With Michalopoulos, we are now investigating at least four crimes," Nikki said. "In addition to his being a murder suspect, he is a suspect in the break-in and attack on me at your house. He's a suspect in the hacking attacks on Involvment.com, for which Michalopoulos' company has a clear motive. Those attacks include the denial-of-service attack and the stealing of the credit card records, two different violations. Where do we start?"

"They are all related, obviously." Archie said. "The motive for murder may be that Hoskins found evidence of the cybercrimes. Or maybe Hoskins just claimed to have evidence, to extort money or other concessions from Michalopoulos to ease his financial condition. Either way, it appears things could have escalated beyond what Hoskins expected. In any case, proving the cybercrimes gives a motive for Michalopoulos to murder Hoskins, and would be part of the case against him. Similarly, it seems clear that the intrusion into my house and the attack on Erasmus are related to the fear that we would uncover the same cybercrimes."

"So perhaps we should start with whether we have proof of the cybercrimes," Nikki said.

"I've asked my contacts at the FBI to dig into this," Archie said, "but it will take a while. They know I'm credible, but they have other competing cases, of course." Archie realized that he should have developed closer friendships with his FBI contacts so that he could press them for priority consideration. Another motivation to improve his social skills, perhaps.

"Let's see what we've uncovered ourselves. Erasmus," Archie said to his smartphone, putting it in speakerphone mode, "What's the status on your Michalopoulos research?"

"As previously reported, statistical analysis suggests that Michalopoulos stole credit card information while working as a security consultant for a number of companies. An analysis of the sales of his first game shows that there was a large spurt in sales immediately when the game was introduced, unusual compared to other games, even successful games. The pattern for successful games is a relatively slow start and then a spurt as word of mouth and recommendations spur further sales. Another anomaly is that an unusually high proportion were credit card sales; it is more typical for low-priced game sales to have more sales through alternative payment methods, such as PayPal."

"Erasmus, pause," Archie said. "Nikki, it sounds almost certain that Michalopoulos launched his first company using stolen credit card numbers. And the money he made from that and the credibility it generated helped him launch Interactive Apps. But we need direct evidence rather than just statistical implications. Erasmus, was there supporting evidence on Michalopoulos' PC or the memory stick?"

"Yes," Erasmus replied. "The memory stick has names and credit card numbers listed under company names. The companies are all companies that Michalopoulos' prior employer lists as clients. The stick was encrypted, but the keys to decryption were on the PC in another file. There were some empty file folders with names that suggested he might have erased the same or similar information from the PC before we examined it."

"I guess he forgot about the memory stick. We can use what you found on it," Nikki said excitedly. "It was obtained under a search warrant. And we can get a warrant for Michalopoulos' employer that lets us see which companies Michalopoulos supposedly 'helped' with their security."

Erasmus continued. "I found no evidence of the hacking of Involvment.com on the PC. I continue to search for such evidence. There was a virus I downloaded that was misidentified as a data file that let me be attacked. I will test each file in the future for suspicious content before I open it. The presence of that file suggests that Michalopoulos was behind the attack on me. He apparently put the virus file on the PC so he could track any penetrations of his PC. End of report."

Archie said, "The virus gives evidence of the attack on Erasmus, and circumstantial evidence of motivation for the intrusion in my house. Well, we seem to have enough evidence to prosecute Michalopoulos for data theft and misuse of credit card data. His labeling of the credit card numbers by company was an obvious error, and seems to bolster the statistical evidence. I'll pass this on to the FBI. Perhaps it will spur faster action."

Nikki thought for a moment. "I'd rather wait to see if we can get more evidence for more of his crimes before we arrest him and he lawyers up. What we have now will probably at least provide enough certainty of a conviction to get an acceptable plea deal on the violations other than murder."

"The accumulation of circumstantial evidence for murder might convince a jury," Archie said.

Nikki looked skeptical. "Beyond a reasonable doubt? Maybe the pathologist has something more. Let's visit him and see if we can get something he didn't think significant enough for a formal report."

She dialed the pathologist, and he said he could see them shortly. They drove to his office.

Chapter 19

Ed Harris, the pathologist that performed the autopsy on Hoskins, greeted them. He said that he thought his report covered all he found, but would be glad to go over it with them.

Nikki asked a question that had been bothering her. "He was shot in the abdomen. He died slowly from blood loss. He tried to reach the phone apparently, judging by the blood trail toward the side table holding it. Why didn't he make it?"

"Perhaps he passed out from blood loss before he made it. I don't think pain would have stopped him. He had a high level of painkiller in his blood."

Archie asked, "High? Higher than prescribed by the doctor?"

"Well, he was supposed to take one tablet two times a day, and the level in his blood was much higher than that dosage would cause. He may have taken two or three at once."

Archie looked puzzled. "Was he in that much pain from the cancer?"

"That's hard to say. His doctor would have objected if he knew about the abuse of the pain medicine, but, given that Hoskins had a relatively short time to live, potential addiction to the medicine was Hoskins' least problem. The doctor would perhaps have noticed when Hoskins tried to renew the prescription early."

"How did you know to look for cancer?" Nikki asked.

"The technical team brought me the medicine from his bathroom drawer. That's how I knew to check for the pain medicine in his blood. I called the doctor that prescribed the medicine, whom I know, and he told me my autopsy should check for pancreatic cancer, which I confirmed. I guess he stretched patient confidentiality by telling me what to look for, as opposed to telling me of the patient's condition."

"Can you say anything about the wound? How close was the gun to the victim when he was shot?" Archie asked.

"Well, it looks like it was very close. There is a lot of gunpowder residue on the victim's clothing and his hands, and the damage is such that it appears like a close shot, perhaps less than a foot away."

"Perhaps Hoskins was trying to take the gun away from the murderer, and it went off, as we speculated," Nikki said.

Archie looked skeptical. "Why would the murderer let him get so close?"

"I agree, it seems strange," Nikki said. "I'm just reviewing the possibilities."

"The gunpowder residue was on both hands?" Archie asked.

"Mostly on the right hand," Harris answered.

They continued going over the results with Harris, but nothing new surfaced. As they left, Nikki asked, "Any new insights?"

"Not really," Archie said. "Just more questions. I wish the evidence made more sense."

Chapter 20

They resisted talking about the case during their next date. Erasmus had suggested an early date at the Getty Museum, which happened to be one of Nikki's favorite places in LA for the exhibits, the architecture, and the location. The sunset was beautiful, with more clouds than usual in LA creating a colorful display. Despite the Getty being far from the ocean, its position at the top of a hill provided a view of the ocean in the distance, making the sunset even more dramatic. "Nature creates art," Nikki said quietly as they stood side by side. Archie took her hand and squeezed it gently. Nikki was a bit surprised, not expecting an emotional response from Archie.

The current special exhibit at the museum was paintings by J.M.W. Turner, an early 19th-century English romanticist landscape painter whose favorite subject was the outdoors and the sky, reminding them of the sunset they had just seen. Erasmus gave his summary of the work of Turner, which was controversial at the time he was alive for being more impressionist than realistic. Erasmus provided more information than they needed, even indicating a Turner painting was in a scene in a museum in a James Bond film, *Skyfall*.

After a quick perusal of the permanent exhibits, they determined to do it again. "It's inspiring," Nikki said.

Archie agreed. "I guess the greatest artists were courageous in trying new ways of expressing themselves, but the subtle message is that the human brain sees things in different ways than computers. We fill in details in our mind, leveraging what we see."

Nikki nodded. "Turner could suggest a sunset or sunrise with a splash of white that sometimes dominated the painting, but you felt what he was seeing."

They went to the restaurant at the museum. The restaurant menu was displayed at the entrance. It was evident why the restaurant did this, signaling high prices and a limited menu. Presumably, the museum architect had provided only a small kitchen.

They looked at the menu, which seemed to feature unusual dishes. "Octopus?" Nikki said. "I suspect there is a reason it's not available in many restaurants."

"Yes," Archie said. "These options seem more different than appetizing."

They decided to go to a casual restaurant on their route to Nikki's apartment that featured sweet potato fries and hamburgers, after determining this was a favorite of both of them. The conversation was relaxed, centering on the source of creativity, and its uniquely human nature. "Creativity that appeals to humans requires growing up in a human body," Nikki said. "It's one area that computers are not likely to conquer."

"They can simulate creativity by copying many examples that humans generated," Archie said. "It's a statistical process that can sometimes produce impressive results when the intention is to replicate what is implicit in the data, but it's derivative by its very nature. Using machine learning, computer software could look at a number of impressionist paintings contrasted with realistic paintings and come up with a simulated impressionist painting that might look like it was done by a human. But true creativity requires invention and a full understanding of human nature, not what is essentially copying."

When they reached her apartment, Nikki asked Archie in for a glass of wine. He rapidly agreed.

They were sitting together on the couch, with Archie inching closer, obviously wondering about a romantic advance. She made it easy for him by reaching up to his face and pulling it closer. Archie kissed her like a man offered a drink of water after a hike through the desert.

Nikki wanted more, but Archie seemed unsure how aggressive to be. She made her permission clear. "Let's go to the bedroom," she said.

They did, kissed again, and began undressing each other. Nikki obviously knew that Archie was slim, but realized that she'd never seen him with his shirt off, and was surprised how muscular he was. He had mentioned coming from the health club a few times and that Erasmus made sure he got enough exercise each day, but she didn't expect what she saw. In turn, Archie looked hungrily at Nikki as he undressed her and said simply, "You're perfect."

He laid her on the bed and felt her all over with a gentle touch. She stroked his body at the same time. Archie couldn't be patient, and began making love to her soon.

Nikki said breathlessly afterward, "Archie, your 'practicing' certainly paid off."

He replied, "I just realized, I was practicing for you."

Archie didn't relax. He turned her on her stomach and gave her a long massage all over her body. He then began making love to her again. "Archie!" she said, surprised.

Archie seemed a bit surprised himself, as he made love to her more slowly than before. "Don't expect this every time," he said. She laughed, despite the distractions.

Later, as she lay with her head on his chest, feeling the particular closeness that sexual intimacy can create, Nikki realized that her doubts about Archie had largely evaporated. She felt it was more than his claims about being a good lover being validated. They slept together all night.

Chapter 21

The next morning, they had coffee and a light breakfast together in Nikki's apartment. Archie needed to go by his condo for fresh clothes for the station. Before leaving, he asked if Nikki felt safe, considering the attack. She said she did, and would be cautious. She reassured Archie, "I don't think another attack would make sense, after we've reported the first. It would just make the connection to the Hoskins case more obvious, and other investigators would be even more aggressive if a police officer were hurt."

After Archie left, Nikki realized she was in a bit of a daze. It hit her that a decision to go on a date or two with Archie to test the waters had led to much more than she expected, and more quickly than she expected.

She had previously gone through a few long-term relationships. They gave way when the physical attraction was overridden by an intellectual disconnect, or an intellectual attraction ran into a physical mismatch. Nikki was smart, and had a job that intimidated some men. Over time, she had decided not to press for relationships when they just weren't there. It wasn't that she decided she was better off alone, but she just didn't want to make finding the right man a major objective of her life. And, despite a good night and Archie's seeming transformation to a warmer personality, she was still a bit skeptical.

She tried to focus on the case at hand. They didn't have a case against Michalopoulos that would likely hold up in court. She took a deep breath, got ready to go to the office, and did so.

Archie arrived at the same time. When he came in, he looked at her without saying anything, just a long stare. Both weren't sure what to say. Nikki smiled and said quietly, "Let's not bring personal things to work, or we won't be able to work."

Archie looked relieved. He had been debating whether he should say what he felt. With Adams already at his nearby desk, that might have been difficult or inappropriate. "OK," he said.

"Where do we stand?" Nikki asked, pointing to the Hoskins file on her desk.

"Well," Archie replied. "We're pretty sure Michalopoulos did some illegal things to make the money that he used to launch the company that destroyed Hoskins' company. It's questionable whether we could create more than a circumstantial case in court unless we can independently find the information that Erasmus found. Erasmus hasn't found a way we can get stronger evidence through more formal legal means. And we don't have evidence that Michalopoulos was behind the hacking attacks on Involvement.com.

"But we now know what Hoskins was suggesting he had over Michalopoulos, even if they were only suspicions. Michalopoulos may have thought Hoskins had, or would find, more, and that provides a motive for murder. And Michalopoulos has admitted he was there the night of the murder.

"But a good defense lawyer—and Michalopoulos can afford one—would simply argue it was revenge against a strong competitor on Hoskins' part, and that Hoskins tried to threaten him without any real evidence, just to extract money. The lawyer would argue that, if Michalopoulos were afraid of even the suggestion of impropriety, he could buy Hoskins off with his company's money, calling it a settlement to avoid a lawsuit. Why kill Hoskins and risk life in prison?"

Nikki nodded. "And killing him wouldn't be likely to solve the problem of Michalopoulos' potential crime being exposed. It might even make it more likely that the possibility of Michalopoulos' wrongdoing would come to light as part of the investigation—as it has."

"Yes," Archie said. "I have trouble with that conundrum myself."

"Perhaps we don't have the right man," Nikki said. "Who else might have done it? Do we have other suspects?"

"We don't, but we've been focusing on Michalopoulos because that's where the evidence initially led." He looked at his smartwatch. "Erasmus, does the data you gathered suggest others that Hoskins might have been in touch with recently?"

"Based on e-mail and mobile phone records, there are others who he has been in contact with in the last week, mostly regarding his financial condition. I'm sending a list with any available contact info and their background to the cloud file on this case."

"Erasmus, which seem most significant to the investigation?"

"Two seem the most significant. One is Joseph Needham, a lawyer specializing in bankruptcy. The other is Floyd Merriweather, who was chief financial officer of Hoskins' company."

Nikki was able to make appointments with Needham later that morning, and Merriweather in the afternoon.

Chapter 22

The lawyer, Joseph Needham, sounded like a lawyer, qualifying most of what he said. He had acted as the lead lawyer in Involvement.com's bankruptcy filing. He summarized, "Involvement.com was doing well in growing the number of users and adding content to the site. Investment banks were expressing a lot of interest in helping with an Initial Public Offering. All was going well, except that the company was adding users and had to invest in more computer power and software to support the growth. And they continued making commitments and paying advances to authors to generate new content and keep users coming back. Hoskins chose to finance this expansion by borrowing huge amounts rather than selling stock in the company to venture firms. The financial institutions lending him money went along with this questionable approach because they all wanted to be involved in the latest big thing, hoping to get a share of the IPO."

Nikki wanted to get to the bottom line. "So the company went bankrupt after competition showed up in the form of Michalopoulos' Interactive Apps, and Involvement.com had the well-publicized hacking and performance issues."

"Yes," Needham said.

"Isn't that bankruptcy a finished deal?" Archie asked.

Needham nodded. "Yes, essentially."

"And did Hoskins get anything out of it personally?" Nikki asked.

"The record of the proceedings show that his interest was essentially wiped out. He got no cash out of the bankruptcy."

Nikki asked, "So why did he call you recently?"

"He was asking me to represent him in his personal bankruptcy case. Apparently, he overspent money personally, anticipating the IPO, which, as you know, didn't happen."

There was a pause. Nikki pressed, "And…"

"I said I didn't do personal bankruptcies. He said some things you might expect, since he gave me the job for the company bankruptcy and felt I owed him something. But I told him I did institutional bankruptcies and didn't feel qualified to handle a personal bankruptcy."

"Did he say anything more?"

"That was pretty much the end of the conversation. It ended on an angry note, with something that sounded like some sort of threat."

Nikki raised an eyebrow. "Can you be more explicit?"

"I don't recall exactly, but he called me an asshole and said something like, 'Remember this conversation. You're responsible for what happens next.'"

"Was he more explicit?" Archie asked.

"No, I just said sorry and hung up."

Nikki also asked about Needham's whereabouts at the time of the murder. He cited a dinner meeting that could be checked.

As they drove to the afternoon appointment, Nikki asked, "I don't see Needham as a suspect."

Archie agreed. He said, "What do you think Hoskins meant by 'what happens next'?"

"It sounds like a suicide threat to me," Nikki said. "I can't see him attacking Needham physically in some way for refusing to be his lawyer, particularly with

Needham claiming lack of competency in individual bankruptcies, even if that was self-serving."

"Perhaps he *was* contemplating suicide," Archie said, "and someone beat him to it."

Chapter 23

Albert Merriweather did have some hard feelings toward Hoskins that he didn't hide. "As CFO, I got a lot of the blame for the bankruptcy. But Hoskins overrode my recommendations that we take in cash as equity investments rather than loans. He ruined my life with his over-optimism and overspending. Not only did it deny me a big payday with an IPO, but it hurt my reputation badly, and is making it difficult to find a comparable position."

"So you killed him," Archie said.

Merriweather looked shocked, realizing he was making himself a suspect. "I don't kill everyone that makes me mad!" he said.

"Just some of them," Nikki said.

Merriweather jumped to his feet. "I didn't mean that!"

Nikki responded coolly, "So where were you the night he was murdered?"

Merriweather thought for a few seconds and looked relieved. "I was having dinner with an executive recruiter who has some clients that might consider me for a job." Nikki took down the name and contact info for the recruiter and the name of the restaurant to check later.

"Do you have any idea who might have murdered him?" Nikki asked.

"Well, he was quite upset with Michalopoulos when our company was going through the downward spiral, and said he had something on Michalopoulos relating to how he'd built his initial fortune."

"His initial fortune? Before Interactive Apps?" Nikki asked.

"Yes," Merriweather replied. "The game company."

"Did Hoskins say anything more specific about that?" Archie asked.

"Just that he couldn't understand how such a boring game could grow so fast, and how Michalopoulos could charge for it when there were better—or at least comparable games—free. He didn't tell me any more about what he suspected."

Archie looked concerned. "Did he indicate that he had any real evidence of malfeasance?"

"No," Merriweather replied. "I thought Edward was just grasping at straws, hoping to be able to fight back against Michalopoulos with equally dirty tactics."

"Equally dirty?" Nikki said. "What was dirty about what Michalopoulos did?"

"Well, he stole the core idea in our service— interactive entertainment. As 'Involvement.com' implies, we took the idea of books and video entertainment and got the reader or watcher involved in the story, impacting the outcome, or at least the progress of the story. People would read our books or watch our video stories over and over to see what happened if they made different choices. We were able to make money by supplying the entertainment as a service with a monthly fee. It particularly appealed to the generations that grew up with interactive games and tended to be bored with passive reading or video watching. Michalopoulos basically stole the idea, making only cosmetic changes."

Archie looked puzzled. "Didn't you have patent protection?"

"We had patents pending, but none granted at the time he launched the service. And, to make matters more painful, Michalopoulos outbid others for the patents pending during the bankruptcy, so they will be his if they are eventually granted."

"OK," Nikki said. "I can see the injustice, but it wasn't illegal. You could have sued him after the patents were granted and perhaps put him out of business, so he was taking a chance. And you had the advantage of being first with the most content, so there shouldn't have been much real competition if you had exploited that position."

"That's what we initially thought, but he began outbidding us for the next content by successful authors—authors we had validated—at a time when our situation was deteriorating due to financial stress and the hacking attacks. The attacks stealing personal information made customers cancel their accounts to protect their credit cards. The denial-of-service attacks meant long waits when the customers interacted with content before the content responded. You can imagine the frustration of users in the middle of a thriller."

"Did you and Hoskins blame Michalopoulos for the hacking attacks?" Archie asked.

"Hoskins was sure it was Michalopoulos, but had no evidence. Of course, Interactive Apps benefited most from the attacks, but I thought Michalopoulos had a lot to lose if he was caught. I felt it might just be the usual hackers showing their power, or thieves that wanted the credit card info. And, of course, one could argue that our CEO, Hoskins, should have spent more resources protecting our security and allocating backup servers—spending more on the IT infrastructure— rather than making growth the only priority, an issue I'm on record as warning him about. Hoskins never answered those criticisms after the fact."

After the meeting, while Nikki drove, a combination of Erasmus finding contact info and Archie making calls validated the alibis of Needham and Merriweather. Erasmus checked Merriweather's financials and found that he had several million dollars in assets accumulated from successes in previous jobs. Archie said, "I can see Merriweather being angry at Hoskins but, particularly since it apparently won't change his lifestyle, not murdering him. If we find some other problems with the relationship, we can double check the alibi, but I don't see further investigation being worthwhile at this point."

Nikki was quiet, thinking about what they might have missed. "Hoskins went through a recent divorce. Maybe there is an insurance policy, with his wife as the beneficiary, something that wouldn't be part of a bankruptcy proceeding. That would make her or someone she hired a suspect."

Archie nodded. "We certainly need to look into that. Most people in that income category have estate lawyers for things like family trusts. The estate lawyer should at least know about any life insurance policies. And the divorce lawyer may know whether the divorce settlement included any life insurance policies. Erasmus, did the records on Hoskins' PC include divorce lawyers or estate lawyers under contacts, or invoices from estate lawyers?"

After a short pause, Erasmus answered, "Yes. The estate lawyer appears to be Cornelius Wells. The divorce lawyer representing Hoskins was Frank Sandson. The ex-wife is Dolores Hoskins. Providing contact info." Archie's mobile phone dinged. Archie was able to get an appointment with the estate lawyer near the end of the day and the divorce lawyer the next morning.

Chapter 24

The estate lawyer, Cornelius Wells, wasn't much help. He wasn't sure if there was a life insurance policy on Hoskins. He said he hadn't recommended one, since, at the time he was retained, Hoskins' stock seemed to be worth tens of millions, and with assets in that amount and a relatively young and healthy individual, he didn't consider life insurance a good investment. He did confirm that most bankruptcy courts would leave alone a life insurance with a beneficiary other than the person undergoing the bankruptcy. Non-payment of premiums would soon cancel the policy in any case.

As they left the attorney's office, there was a bit of unspoken tension between Archie and Nikki. Their relationship was at a point where it was definitely a "thing," but Archie didn't know how hard to push, and Nikki was uncomfortable about establishing the connection too quickly as a long-term relationship. She was still wondering about whether it could work out long-term. And she was only assuming Archie wanted it to; she really didn't know his attitude about commitment. It was obvious he enjoyed the sex.

She decided to go slow and broke the silence. "I have a few things to catch up on tonight—bills and such, so I'll just drop you off at your car."

Archie looked disappointed. "OK," he said.

He looked so disturbed that Nikki thought perhaps he was taking it as a rejection, something she certainly didn't intend. "Archie, I'd like to take you in my arms right now, but I want to go slow in our relationship."

He looked relieved. "OK, I'm not used to feeling the way I do. I don't know how much I should push. Nikki, I don't know how to explain my feelings."

"I feel the same way, Archie," she replied. "Our relationship changed so quickly, I think we both need time to make sure it's real."

"OK," Archie said, but was apparently not happy with moving slowly. "I'll see you in the morning," he said as they arrived at the headquarters garage.

Chapter 25

Edward Hoskins' divorce lawyer, Frank Sandson, was cooperative the next day. He indicated that the divorce proceedings were unfriendly. Dolores had left Edward with no warning, trucking out all of her possessions and a number of assets in the house, such as paintings and other items of value. She also transferred whatever was in joint bank or savings accounts to her individual accounts.

Sandson said that Dolores was in some sense a trophy wife, one Hoskins had married after his apparent success with Involvement.com; a young and beautiful woman, and Edward had been deeply hurt by her apparent clear interest in his money, rather than him. The divorce negotiations came after it was obvious that Edward was approaching bankruptcy. In the end, Dolores was left with whatever she had taken. Sandson said that it was pointless for him to claim the assets she had taken were his, since that would cost him substantial legal fees, even if successful, and success would only mean more money for his creditors.

He said there was a life insurance policy with Dolores Hoskins as sole beneficiary, but it required monthly payments, and Edward had stopped paying, perhaps intending to void the policy. The divorce agreement didn't require him to continue paying installments, and he couldn't in any case. The lawyer wasn't sure what the terms of the policy were, and how long it would be until the policy was cancelled, but he didn't think Edward bothered to formally cancel it. Divorce negotiations had taken place about three months prior, and the final papers hadn't yet been filed. Legally, she was his widow, not his divorced wife. If the policy hadn't been cancelled, she would be the beneficiary.

Erasmus had the insurance company, the policy number, and even a username and password for the insurance company website that he'd found in a spreadsheet called "Important numbers" on Hoskins' PC. Archie used the information to log in to the Hoskins account on the website. It showed the policy in good standing; apparently, someone had been making the monthly payments. Erasmus was able to track the payments to a bank account in Dolores Hoskins' name.

"More than interesting," Nikki said, when Archie indicated what he had found. "I guess we have another suspect. And this is someone Hoskins would have let into his house, I presume, if she claimed to have a change of heart or some business to discuss with him."

They were able to arrange to visit Dolores Hoskins at her apartment that afternoon.

Chapter 26

Dolores Hoskins was, as described, an attractive woman. She was slim, and dressed to show off an impressive figure. Nikki was curious about Archie's reaction. He went through the usual male visual assessment of a woman, but didn't seem impressed. Nikki didn't know it, but Archie didn't like women who were taken with their own looks, and Dolores seemed to expect adoration from men by her posture and dress without saying a word. Archie associated such obsession with physical characteristics with a lack of intelligence; most intelligent, attractive women like Nikki seemed to be put off by others focusing on how they appeared.

Nikki started with a condolence. "We're sorry about the death of your husband, Ms. Hoskins."

"Just call me Dolores. As you probably know, we were divorcing, so I'm not truly grieving."

Nikki didn't react to the callous statement. "Did you see him recently?"

"Not since two weeks ago, when we met with our divorce lawyers to hammer out details of the settlement. Not that Edward had any assets left to talk about. I guess the death makes the finalization of the divorce unnecessary."

"I understand he had a life insurance policy payable to you," Archie said, impatient to get to the point.

Dolores didn't flinch. "Yes, he did. Not too big a one, but it will compensate me somewhat for the time I wasted with him. Fortunately, I talked him into the policy despite his trust lawyer saying it wasn't necessary. Insurance is insurance. At the time, the premiums didn't seem like enough for him to argue about."

"Wasn't the policy cancelled when he stopped making monthly payments?" Archie said.

"When he got into financial trouble," she said, "I called the insurance company and had them deliver the bills to a P.O. Box so I could make sure the monthly payments were made."

"He didn't cancel the policy?" Nikki asked.

"He didn't think of it after he stopped getting the bills. I suppose he figured that the insurance company dropped him for non-payment."

Archie, not strong on subtlety, said, "How did you know he would die?"

"Didn't someone say, 'In the long run, we're all dead'?"

"Yes," Archie said. "John Maynard Keynes. He was talking economics. We're talking murder."

She looked shocked, as if she just realized she might be a suspect. "I just thought I'd try keeping it for a while. I wanted to salvage something from this mess. He was pretty stressed out. I thought he might have a heart attack over the failure of his firm."

"Warm thoughts," Nikki said. "Where were you the night he died?"

"I was out on a date."

Archie handed her his phone. "Would you please enter the name and contact information of the person you were with?" She did, entering David Goldsmith and a phone number on the note pad, looking significantly more nervous than at the beginning of the conversation.

"How late were you out?" Nikki asked.

She looked relieved. "All night. I spent the night at his condo in the city."

Archie said, "Can we look at your calendar on your mobile phone to validate the engagement?"

She uncomfortably took out her smartphone and handed it to him, starting it up with a fingerprint reader. Without saying anything, Archie attached it to his phone with a cable from his pocket and said, "Erasmus, check it out."

"Wait," she said, trying to take the phone back.

"I'm just taking a look at your calendar," Archie said. "Erasmus, what's the calendar entry for the date of the Hoskins murder?"

"A hair appointment in the afternoon and a dinner date with Dave Goldsmith at 7 PM. He was to pick her up at her apartment at that time."

"I guess that settles it," Archie said. "Erasmus, are you done?"

"Download complete," was the answer. Dolores looked puzzled, but took her phone back without comment after Archie disconnected it.

They asked a few more questions that might lead to associates or friends who might know someone who would murder for hire, but nothing developed. They left.

As they drove away, Archie said, "Erasmus, see who Dolores Hoskins recently contacted and list the content of those contacts." He said to Nikki, "Maybe we'll get lucky. She didn't seem too bright. Erasmus, send contact information for her date Dave Goldsmith to Nikki."

"I'll check out the alibi," Nikki said. "But I don't see her killing her ex-husband in person. She'd be the prime suspect if the insurance policy were found."

"But she didn't seem too bright," Archie repeated.

An uncomfortable silence followed. Archie realized that there couldn't be a decision each day about whether they got together that night, sensing that Nikki was not ready for a full commitment, although he'd like it to be that simple. So he said, "How about dinner somewhere tomorrow?"

"That sounds good," Nikki said. She felt relieved that she didn't have to make a decision about tonight, but also relieved that there was a firm "next time," and, she realized, happy that it was soon.

Chapter 27

The next day, Nikki confirmed by phone that Goldsmith had dinner with Dolores, confirming with him and with the restaurant. They also checked out Goldsmith's background, and found that he was a relatively wealthy businessman, and unlikely to have any motivation to help Dolores kill her soon-to-be ex-husband. It didn't appear that the relationship would last. "That was our first and last date," Goldsmith said, declining to explain how he'd met her. Erasmus confirmed that there was no earlier calendar entry or e-mail exchanges for Goldsmith on Dolores' calendar. Erasmus also revealed that data from her mobile phone revealed they met through a Web dating service.

"Can Erasmus check how much the life insurance policy was for?" Nikki asked.

"There should have been a digital or paper copy somewhere. Erasmus, does any data from Edward Hoskins show a life insurance policy and its amount?"

After a short pause, Erasmus said, "There is a record of a policy for ten million, but some e-mail warnings about monthly payments due."

"Erasmus, any notification of termination?"

"No," Erasmus said, "And the warnings of termination ceased three months ago."

"That was about the time Dolores sued for divorce," Nikki noted.

"I guess she had a ten-million-dollar motivation for murder," Archie said. "Erasmus delivered contacts he could find on her smartphone and in a service in the cloud that she used for storing backup of her data. He could get into it with information in the phone—I guess she assumed no one would have access to her phone. I have a long list arranged by date from contacts she called or messaged most currently to older ones. Erasmus analyzed the nature of the contacts as best he could from messages on the phone and whatever other information he could find about the contacts independently. Some are obvious and unlikely suspects—for example, her divorce lawyer."

Nikki looked skeptical. "Let's not eliminate suspects too quickly. The divorce lawyer may have been promised a cut of the $10 million if he helped her, and a lawyer may have represented some unsavory characters. He may not have only done divorce law in his career, or might have helped some unsavory characters through a divorce."

"Good point," Archie said. "I guess we have to pay him a visit. His name is Charles Hughes. I'll look through Erasmus' list for other possibilities."

Archie abruptly changed the subject. "I'd like to cook dinner for you tonight at my place."

"That's not necessary, Archie. I didn't even know you cooked."

"I have a few things I've practiced."

Nikki smiled. "Well, I've learned that you do well with 'practice,' so how can I resist?"

"Do you like Indian food?" Archie asked. She did.

Nikki went home to change, and Archie went shopping for his ingredients. Nikki said she'd drive over, since Archie would be cooking. He continued to surprise her.

Chapter 28

The dinner Archie served rivaled a fancy restaurant. The main course was Chicken Tikka Masala, a spicy dish, served with side dishes and wine. "Archie, how did you do this so fast?" Nikki asked. "It's wonderful. If I cook for you, I guess I can't just order take-out."

"Take-out is my usual meal, actually," Archie said. "If I cook for you much, you'll see that my repertoire is limited. But I've cooked my specialties enough that I've become pretty efficient at it. For example, I have jars of pre-apportioned spices for Chicken Masala."

"That sounds like you, Archie. I'll have to develop some specialties. I certainly like this dish."

Archie said, "It's one of my favorites. One story has it that Chicken Tikka Masala was invented by accident in a UK restaurant. A patron eating Chicken Curry complained that there wasn't enough sauce and asked them to add his tomato soup to the Chicken Curry. The patron liked it so much that the restaurant added it to the menu, with a few enhancements. I'm not sure how the dish spread or if this story is accurate, but Chicken Tikka Marsala is certainly now a staple of most Indian restaurants."

Nikki said, "I haven't been motivated to cook much, since it's usually for myself. I usually see my friends at some occasion where there is food or drinks, and I don't have any family locally."

"Have your dates cooked for you, or you cooked for them in the past?" Archie asked.

Nikki smiled. She hadn't discussed her social life to any extent with Archie in the past, and he was clearly curious, perhaps wondering if he had current competition. "Well, I've had a few serious relationships in the past, but they didn't work out. Cooking for each other was an unusual event."

She decided to answer what she thought was Archie's real question. "In the last couple of years, I got turned off on the dating scene. Maybe because of what I do, I've realized some of the dangers involved. Or, maybe because of what I do, some men I'd want to date don't want to get involved, so I'm not meeting men that intrigue me. Dating just for sex isn't an attractive option. I go to some events and parties with friends, but not always with a date. I recently turned 30, and I must admit it has led to some soul-searching about how I want the rest of my life to turn out."

She realized she didn't know much about Archie's social life. "What about you? Have you done much serious dating?"

Archie looked as if he were trying to analyze the question. "Well, sometimes I'm encouraged when a woman smiles at me, but I don't know how to engage with them without seeming strange, apparently. I like to talk about intellectual topics, but it's hard to start a conversation with something like, 'What do you think about the Higgs Boson?' I tried the dating services online. I looked at how other men described themselves on the website and got some idea of how to make myself interesting. I used a photo that made me look good, and the combination created some activity. I got a number of inquiries from women, and went out on some dates. Some resulted in sex, but I didn't go on more than a couple of dates with women that initiated the contact, for a number of reasons. I initiated contact with some women that looked attractive and interesting, and that went better, since I picked women who seemed to have intellectual interests. But I guess I should have taken lessons from Erasmus on social interactions earlier, because the ones I dated long enough to meet their friends said in effect that their friends thought I was strange."

"You never introduced a female friend to me," Nikki said.

"I didn't want you to think I had a girlfriend," Archie said, looking a bit embarrassed. "And, you know now that I wanted more than a business relationship, but you seemed to discourage that, so I assumed you had a romantic attachment, and I only recently admitted my interest to you."

"Well," Nikki said, "We certainly have some common interests in our work. But I hope we develop more beyond solving murders."

"There's always sex," Archie said, apparently seriously.

Nikki smiled. "So far, so good," she said.

Bringing up the subject seemed to inspire some thoughts in that direction, and they finished their wine quickly. Archie looked uncomfortable and at a loss for words, so Nikki made it easy. "Can you show me your bedroom?" she asked coyly.

"My pleasure," Archie said.

The lovemaking proceeded more slowly this time, less driven by the urgency that characterized the first time. Afterward, Nikki whispered, "So far, so good."

Chapter 29

Nikki called Charles Hughes, Dolores' divorce lawyer, the next day. He said he couldn't talk to her and Archie—attorney-client privilege.

Archie did what he usually did to find information when it wasn't forthcoming—he asked Erasmus. Erasmus found that the divorce had proceeded through discovery stages, and that it became clear that Hoskins would be bankrupt soon. "Hughes doesn't try to protect his records from hacking in any noticeable way," Archie said. "So much for attorney-client privilege."

They also learned from open sources that Hughes had started his career in the public defender's office, and had represented a number of violent criminals. Those could be individuals Dolores hired through the lawyer, if he was indeed involved. Erasmus was able to find those cases, and provided information about the criminals that had been accused of violent crimes. To do a complete job of that, Erasmus used the back channel to the NSA that Archie had installed. The NSA software was not, in theory, used to investigate individuals in the US, but Archie could use it for that purpose through the secret access.

Archie tried to use the NSA conduit as a last resource, to avoid calling attention to it by too much activity. While at the Agency, he'd set up a program that periodically made an inquiry to an outside server he'd set up. Since the inquiry was started from inside the Agency and completely encrypted, the Agency firewall would neither block nor analyze the communication. Archie had set up the software at the Agency so that it periodically replicated itself to different servers, in case some servers were erased or shut down. The connection established in this way could then be used to access internal databases and tools, although that required insider knowledge Archie had gained while at the Agency. Since Archie's database inquiries always passed through at least one other Agency computer and never changed any data in Agency databases, the intrusion would look like any other internal inquiry to the database server. And the servers on Archie's end were intermediaries that, if enough links were traced back, would connect through various Eastern European and Southeast Asian countries, with none of those countries respecting the Agency's jurisdiction. Any attempt to trace the purchases of these services or devices would lead back to one of a handful of dementia patients who may or may not have since passed away. Additionally, several of these devices were encrypted, and would delete their own keys—rendering them unreadable even to Archie—if someone other than Erasmus attempted to analyze their programming and the few logs they stored of past activity.

Hughes hadn't stayed in the public defender's office for long, and hadn't been particularly good at it, judging from the outcome of his cases. He had moved from that job to an entry job at a firm specializing in divorce fairly quickly, so there weren't too many cases to examine. Only two of those individuals were still in LA and not in jail at the time of Hoskins' murder. Only one seemed to have a record with sufficient violence to suggest Hughes could approach him to be a hired murderer. His name was Eric Hansen; he had a previous conviction for battery, for which he'd served time. In the case where Hansen represented him, Hansen seriously injured a friend during a fight. Hughes argued self-defense, and there wasn't sufficient evidence to disprove that contention. Hansen had some injuries himself, making self-defense more credible. The prosecutor argued that those injuries were self-inflicted to make self-defense credible when Hughes thought the victim was dead and knew that it could be proved they were together at the location of the assault, but the argument didn't convince a jury.

Nikki found that Hansen, who was still on parole from an earlier offense, was working at a delivery service loading trucks. Archie and Nikki went there during the day when he'd be expected to be working, and indeed found him there. A supervisor allowed him to stop working to talk to the police.

Hansen wasn't happy. "You're going to cost me my job," he said.

"We apologize for the interruption, and we'll keep it short," Nikki said. "We understand that you were at the home of Edward Hoskins last Tuesday, and wondered what you were doing there."

"Who the hell is Edward Hoskins?!" Hansen exclaimed. "What are you talking about?"

"We know you were there," Nikki bluffed. "Why?"

"Where is 'there'?" Hansen said. "And when?"

"Where is 980 Moorpark Road in Beverly Hills, and when is last Tuesday."

Hansen was honestly puzzled, or at least a good actor. "I can't even remember the last time I've been to Beverly Hills! It's not exactly my neighborhood. And, last Tuesday? I was working here all day."

"What about the evening?" Nikki asked.

He thought a moment. "I went home and watched the basketball game, I think."

"Who was playing?" Archie asked.

"Michigan and UCLA," he said. "Lousy game. UCLA lost." Archie was typing something into his smartphone. He nodded. "Yep, low-scoring game."

"What are you talking about?" Hansen said. "There was almost no defense on either side. I'm surprised there was a net left with all the dunks in that game."

Archie shrugged. "I guess I'm remembering it wrong." Nikki realized that Archie was testing Hansen's claim of having watched the game.

"Do you know Charles Hughes?" Nikki asked, abruptly changing the subject.

"You mean the lawyer? He defended me a while back," Hansen replied.

"When was the last time you talked to him?"

"I haven't talked to him since the case was settled. I haven't needed a lawyer since then, and I don't want to ever need one again. And it will help if I can keep this job. I don't know what the hell you want from me, but you're on the wrong track. I have no idea what you're talking about, and I'd like to get back to work."

Nikki looked at Archie, and he said nothing. Nikki said, "Thanks for your time, Mr. Hansen. Sorry to have bothered you. We appreciate your time."

Somewhat mollified, Hansen said, "OK, good-bye."

As they left, Archie said, "Unless he's a very good actor, there wasn't anything there to suggest he did the deed. And the fact that he was so concerned about his job suggests he didn't recently come into a large sum of money."

"The relationship to Dolores Hoskins was pretty tenuous to begin with. And that leaves us with nothing but dead ends," Nikki said. "We may have to return to Hansen, but we need to think this through and see where we are."

"Speaking of where we are," Archie said, "I don't know how fast to push our relationship. The way I feel right now, I'd like to be with you every night."

Nikki thought a moment. "Archie, I must admit, I feel the same way. But both of us are used to a lot of

105

time to ourselves in the evenings, and we do see each other most days. I don't want to hurt what seems to be developing by pushing it too fast." She paused in thought. "And, given that I'm saying we shouldn't yet make it an everyday thing, it seems uncomfortable to make it a daily decision. Do you want to set up some sort of default schedule to make it simpler? Open to revision, of course."

"That makes sense," Archie said. "How about Monday through Sunday?"

Nikki laughed. "How about a couple of days a week for now?"

"OK," Archie said. "How about Wednesday, Friday, and Saturday?"

Nikki laughed. "I guess you define 'a couple of days' differently than most. OK, it's a date, or rather several dates a week." Nikki said. She wondered how this had happened so quickly, and why she wasn't more skeptical.

Chapter 30

Nikki and Archie discussed the case the next day, concluding that they had no clear routes forward to prove that Michalopoulos murdered Hoskins. "We should pursue the other crimes he may have committed—the apparent fraud in stealing credit cards and the hacking of Hoskins' company," Archie suggested. "Perhaps we can get enough there to at least build that part of the case. If we can show that Hoskins' notes suggesting that he was going to confront Michalopoulos had any substance, we may at least have a motive for Michalopoulos shutting him up."

"And, of course, we may at least be able to convict Michalopoulos of those crimes," Nikki noted.

"The difficulty," Archie said, "is that much of what Erasmus discovers may have to be replicated under a court order to make it admissible evidence."

"I understand," Nikki said. "We do have the data from the memory stick that shows credit cards under company names that were companies he did security work for. That's pretty damning, and was obtained under a search warrant."

"That could justify an arrest, but I'd rather have more ammunition first, given that he's going to fight this with top lawyers that might find a way to interpret that information differently or find a way to disallow it. I checked with the FBI, and they are digging into it, finally. No results yet. But we could go back to the roots, and see if we can get anything showing he stole credit card numbers while at the security company."

"Where would we start?"

Archie pondered the options. "How about associates at the security company? He may have needed cooperation from someone else. I can't imagine a security company not being a bit paranoid and having at least two employees required to work on sensitive data together." He paused. "Erasmus, who worked closely with George Michalopoulos at National Security Solutions?"

Erasmus replied surprisingly quickly. "I have that data based on earlier requests. He was assigned to the same companies at the same time as Fred Oberteuffer. They seem to have worked together as a team. Oberteuffer seems to be retired. His current contact information has been delivered to your phone."

"Erasmus, you never cease to amaze me," Nikki said.

"Thank you," Erasmus replied. "Just doing my job."

Archie looked at the data on his phone. "We have a local home address. Should we just show up and surprise him, or try to make an appointment?"

"He may not be there," Nikki said. "But surprise is the best policy, if possible."

On the way to Oberteuffer's house, Archie had Erasmus investigate him further.

Chapter 31

Oberteuffer answered the door at his house. He looked nervous when Nikki announced she was with the police department. His first response was, "Do I need a lawyer?"

Nikki said smoothly, "Well, that's up to you, but we're here to ask about a colleague. You only need a lawyer if you have something to hide."

The suggestion that he would look guilty if he didn't cooperate had the desired effect. "OK, come in, but I don't have much time, so let's make it quick." He motioned them toward his living room, and they sat down.

Nikki started. "I believe you worked with George Michalopoulos at National Security Solutions." She paused, making it a question.

"Yes," Oberteuffer said, with no elaboration.

"You worked as a team on most jobs," Archie said, making it a fact. Oberteuffer was silent. Archie continued, "Did you and Michalopoulos have access to confidential information at those firms?"

Oberteuffer squirmed, obviously considering how to answer. "Only what was necessary to do our jobs."

"That included customer data, I presume?"

"We had to know where it was and how it was protected. We were there to make sure it was adequately protected. That was our job."

Nikki asked, "I presume you worked in pairs so that there wouldn't be any temptation to inappropriately access data, such as credit card data."

Oberteuffer hesitated, saying nothing, but looking uncomfortable. Nikki said, "Is that a hard question?"

"I don't know what the company's motivation for our working in teams was," he said. "But I couldn't watch every move George made. He wasn't the type to do anything illegal though. He's a successful businessman now, as you certainly know."

"Successful businessmen occasionally commit crimes," Nikki said. "We know he stole credit card information from multiple companies. Here's a list." She pulled from her purse a list of the companies listed on the memory stick they had obtained at Michalopoulos' house and showed it to Oberteuffer. He was obviously taken aback.

"Those are all companies where you worked together," Archie said, stating it as a fact, based on Erasmus' data.

Oberteuffer knew this could be validated. "Yes, but I don't know anything about credit card numbers."

Archie used data Erasmus had found on the way over. "So this has nothing to do with the large amounts of money you deposited in Swiss bank accounts after Michalopoulos started his game company?"

Oberteuffer looked shocked. He was silent.

Nikki said, "Mr. Oberteuffer, just putting money in a Swiss account isn't a crime, but I suspect you didn't pay taxes on that money either, and would have a hard time explaining where it came from. You can just ignore the trouble you're in, or you can tell what you know about Michalopoulos' activity, and we'll offer you a deal."

Oberteuffer looked ill. "Are you OK?" Nikki said.

"I'd better talk to my lawyer and get back to you," he said.

They took that to mean he would incriminate Michalopoulos, and set up a time to meet him and his lawyer at police headquarters.

Chapter 32

Michalopoulos was willing to come to the station and talk when threatened with arrest as an alternative. Nikki thought that he would, since he would be curious as to what charge they would be arresting him on. Of course, he showed up with his lawyer. She was an attractive woman, with long reddish hair, looking like and dressed like a model. Michalopoulos introduced her. "This is my lawyer, Katherine Murphy."

Nikki noticed that Archie surveyed more than her face when she arrived. Murphy addressed Archie first. "It's a pleasure to meet you, Mr. Teal," she said, extending her hand. "I've heard about your accomplishments—very impressive." Archie shook her hand, and Nikki couldn't help noticing that Murphy held the handshake longer than necessary. Archie said, "Thank you. Nice to meet you." Apparently, he was practicing his new social skills, Nikki thought, hoping he didn't mean it literally.

"And I assume you are Detective Sharp," she said, offering a much briefer handshake.

Michalopoulos looked impatient. "I don't know why I'm here. I don't have much to say, and may not say anything if my lawyer so advises."

Nikki thought about the fiber she had after the attack at Archie's place and decided that starting with an aggressive bluff might elicit a response. "Mr. Michalopoulos," she said, with no preface, "I have a part of your jacket I ripped off when you attacked me. We have a warrant to compare the tear with your jacket."

Michalopoulos looked annoyed, and ignored Murphy's motions not to answer. "Nonsense," he said. "My jacket isn't torn."

"I see," Nikki said. "So you admit you attacked me."

Michalopoulos looked panicked. He hadn't actually admitted anything, but realized his response was inappropriate. "I just mean I don't have any torn jackets."

"Not even your brown jacket?"

"I wasn't wearing my brown jacket!" Michalopoulos blurted. His lawyer grabbed his arm. "I mean, I *never* wear my brown jacket," he said, more sheepishly.

Nikki smiled. "No, I guess it was your black one. It didn't tear but I got some fibers from it, and they have your DNA on it. But we don't want to just charge you with breaking and entering, interfering with a police investigation, and attacking a police officer, given all the other crimes you've committed." There wasn't actually any DNA on the fiber, but she wanted to see if she could provoke a response.

Murphy interrupted. "I don't think we should talk further."

"What other crimes?" Michalopoulos said. "I didn't even go in Hoskins' house!"

Archie piped in, "Oh, we aren't even talking about that—yet. We're talking first about your theft of credit card numbers when at National Security Solutions. Of course, you know we have the memory stick we picked up under search warrant in your house, where you made the mistake of labeling the credit card numbers stolen by the company from which you stole them."

Michalopoulos had some explanation prepared, apparently, and started to speak, but a motion from his attorney silenced him.

Archie continued. "And your friend, Fred Oberteuffer, decided it was better to tell on you if it meant a reduced sentence." Michalopoulos started, obviously not expecting this.

Murphy said, "Enough. I don't think my client should cooperate any further."

Nikki said, "We didn't expect him to. The FBI has other evidence, and will be in touch. They'll be taking over this case." That wasn't a bluff; the FBI had uncovered some independent evidence on the credit card theft and, with Nikki's and Archie's evidence, particularly if Oberteuffer testified as part of a plea deal, actually had a solid case.

Michalopoulos and his lawyer started to leave. Archie said, "And, of course, there is the hacking of a competitor. There are a long list of laws that could apply to that. We'll have proof of your involvement soon. Perhaps you should attempt a plea deal before things get worse."

Michalopoulos had frozen as Archie said this. He looked shaken. Archie was pretty sure he would discuss how he could minimize the damage with his lawyer.

Nikki couldn't resist a final arrow. "And of course there is the murder of Edward Hoskins."

Michalopoulos couldn't keep quiet. "I didn't do that! He obviously set me up!" He turned to leave. Murphy started to follow but, as an apparent afterthought, returned and gave Archie her business card. "Perhaps we can meet in a less adversarial context after this is over," she said, smiling. Archie took her card with no comment, a bit nonplussed, as she followed Michalopoulos.

Nikki realized that she was jealous. The woman would fit Archie's criterion of being intelligent as well as attractive. The encounter made her realize that, because Archie had been the initiator of their relationship, she had been taking him for granted, controlling the relationship in a way that suggested continuing the relationship was entirely her option. It hit her that she would be deeply hurt if she lost Archie, and she should act on that realization. Archie's social skills were evolving to make him more charming, although that adjective was still a bit of a stretch. She also realized he was dressing better for work, looking more stylish since they had begun dating. Perhaps with some advice from Erasmus?

She was silent as Michalopoulos and Murphy left, pondering this insight. Finally, Archie said, "It's interesting that he denied the murder so vociferously. Maybe he really didn't do it."

"And maybe he did," Nikki said, relieved that Archie was thinking about the investigation instead of Murphy.

Chapter 33

The weekend came, and it was date time per the pre-arranged schedule. Nikki felt a bit uncomfortable with having set such limits after her realization that it implied she was controlling the interaction, taking Archie for granted. She decided to encourage a less formal evening to show that the relationship wasn't one-sided. While they were working, trying to put all the pieces together in the investigation, including documenting their encounter with Oberteuffer and reporting it to the FBI, she raised the question of that evening before Archie could.

"Archie, why don't we keep tonight simple. Come over to my house. We'll order a pizza and watch a movie on TV. And bring a change of clothes so that you can stay over, and we can spend the day together Saturday."

Archie looked a bit surprised, but happy. "That sounds great to me," Archie said. "I like pizza." His social skills training sounded an alarm. "And being with you," he added quickly. It wasn't just a polite statement.

That evening went as planned, including the implicit invitation to spend the night together. Nikki surprised Archie by changing into sexy lingerie before getting into bed with him, and showed her appreciation of Archie's skills with some of her own. It was a good night, and they slept late the next morning. Nikki realized she had never felt so comfortable with a man. Archie's attitude showed in uncharacteristic fond gestures, with impulsive hugs and gentle touches the next morning. Nikki didn't think Erasmus taught Archie the underlying emotions behind those gestures.

They went for brunch in Santa Monica, and then took a long walk in Palisades Park, a long, thin park on a cliff overlooking the beach. While walking, they passed a rose garden and talked of the recurring drought in California, water shortages, and global warming, acknowledging the downside of the beautiful weather. Both followed the news and were interested in complex topics, so there was little difficulty in finding subjects to talk about. If they had a question about one of the issues, Erasmus was more than willing to participate in the conversation.

Later in the afternoon, they relaxed at a coffee shop in the area, reading different sections of the paper and talking. Both relaxed through reading, so they were able to do so together without it seeming impolite. But the question of their relationship hung in the air, and Nikki decided to bring it up while they sat in the coffee shop.

"Archie, I feel that our relationship has developed well beyond dating. I love being with you outside work in every way. I want you to know that."

Archie looked at her warmly and squeezed her hand. "Thank you for saying that. I haven't felt this way before in my life, and I now understand what all these movies and books talking about love mean. I was comfortable being alone before, but I don't know how I could go back to that. I guess I've loved you for a long time, but our closer relationship has taught me what that really means."

Nikki felt tears coming to her eyes. "I thought I knew what love meant. I've had some passionate relationships and some compelling friendships, but this is the first time the two seemed to coincide. So I guess you could say I've come to understand what love means as well."

They both looked at each other, not sure what to say next. Nikki eventually said, "I guess I'm frightened that something will go wrong. I'm naturally cautious—part of the job, perhaps—and that led me to ask you to go slow. I don't want to set rules anymore. Dating by the calendar isn't very romantic."

Archie still felt at a loss for words, but tried. "I feel I can't get enough of you, so I'm afraid of overwhelming you. We both are used to a lot of time to ourselves, but we can decide to allow ourselves personal time for relaxing or working, even when we are together."

Nikki said, "I think that's the key. We have to understand we can be together without feeling we have to be entertaining each other constantly when we are. And, on the other hand, we have a partner to enjoy things with rather than doing them alone." She was thinking of the tickets to a concert at the Hollywood Bowl that evening that they had agreed upon. She added, feeling a bit self-conscious about the conversation, "And we don't have to overanalyze what we feel."

Archie laughed. "Are you saying we don't have to rationalize what we don't yet understand? But certainly enjoy?"

Nikki laughed, "I guess so."

They enjoyed the concert that evening—and what followed at Nikki's place. The next morning, Nikki said, as they planned their activities for Sunday, "I guess you should leave some clothes and toiletries here."

Archie beamed.

Chapter 34

Archie and Nikki communicated with the FBI regarding Oberteuffer. Archie said they smelled a deal where Oberteuffer would testify against Michalopoulos on the credit card theft and gave what they had, including a summary of the interview, to the FBI. Associated with the credit card theft was the possibility of accounting fraud with the game company. For further leverage, they told the FBI that they may have frightened Michalopoulos re the burglary and assault, and it could be leverage in a negotiated deal. The FBI, at this point, smelled a strong high-publicity case against a well-known executive, and was moving quickly. They claimed to have some supporting independent evidence of their own on the credit card case, as well as some evidence of income tax evasion by Michalopoulos. Archie also told the FBI of their suspicions about the hacking attacks on Involvement.com and on Erasmus, but couldn't provide more evidence than a motive. They hoped the FBI's resources might be able to find something.

"On the murder, we should keep looking at all the alternatives," Nikki said. "I'm still not convinced Michalopoulos did it."

"What about the wife?" Archie asked. "We tried one route where she might have found someone to kill Hoskins for her that didn't pan out, or apparently so. That's not exactly definitive. And she certainly had a multi-million-dollar motive."

Nikki said, "The wife is a good actor, or just smart about not trying to hide her interest in his death. But what other suspects do we have?"

"If Dolores hired the killer, a person with no other motive than a payday, we'd have to trace him through whoever hired him—or her. We haven't found any physical evidence at the crime scene or video from the area we can use to identify such a person. Erasmus has dug into that with what he has, but I can ask him to dig deeper. We may need a search warrant to get into Dolores' PC or other sources at her house."

"I should be able to do that, given she paid insurance premiums surreptitiously. I'll request it when we get back to the station."

"And get a warrant for her home phone records," Archie added.

Chapter 35

Although she didn't want to assume it was her decision alone about continuing the relationship with Archie, Nikki felt uncomfortable because of the speed and depth of the developing relationship. She was afraid it was too good to be true, and something would go wrong. They hadn't had an argument yet, and somehow that frightened her. They couldn't agree on everything, and she felt that fair disagreements were a part of a good and honest relationship.

The relationship had evolved to the point that a "date" wasn't necessary for every encounter. Sometimes she would just go home with Archie, or vice versa. Both had now left clothes and toiletries at each other's place, and each evening they were together, they spent the night. One night, on such an informal evening, she felt she had to test the relationship a bit deeper.

"Archie, don't get this wrong, but I'm curious how you feel about children."

"I like children," Archie said. "I have a few relatives with children, but I don't have too much contact with them."

"I meant having your own children."

Archie looked a bit taken aback. "I guess I never really thought about it. I was never in a relationship that led me to consider it a possibility." He looked surprised. "I guess I am now. But shouldn't we get married first?"

Nikki laughed. "Wow! Is that a proposal? I just wondered what you thought about children in the abstract."

"It's hard to consider that an abstract concept. I can't have children alone. Well, I guess I could adopt as a single father, but I never considered it. It seems for me to be part of a relationship with a woman, not something separate. So I guess the real question revolves around whether you would want to have children."

"So you would father children if it was something I wanted?"

"Of course."

"That response bothers me. I wouldn't want to have children if the father was doing it as a favor to me. Children are a huge responsibility and bring a new dimension to a relationship."

"You're not being fair," Archie said. "I'm a logical person, and tend to take things one at a time. I have been thinking about being married to you, but I was afraid it was too soon to even suggest it. I hope we are moving toward living together, to be frank. This deciding whose place to go to each night is getting a bit annoying. It seemed like a decision about children was far enough in the future that I haven't thought much about it. But it does make sense, I guess, to see if we have consistent feelings about what could become an eventual question."

"Archie, if I'm honest, living together seems like the next step to me also. But things have moved so fast that I feel like we may somehow be kidding ourselves. The sex is fantastic, and perhaps it's driving everything else. I've always felt that I wanted to live together with someone before a stronger commitment, so I'm glad you're thinking similarly, but that's not why I asked the question. I want to understand you better, and that is a longer-term question that we should discuss just for the purpose of understanding. Children involve a serious level of socializing at a different level than I think Erasmus can help you with."

"Of course. I'm aware that children involve tasks that aren't all pleasant, from changing diapers to dealing with temper tantrums. And it's necessary to provide a healthy, loving environment they can grow up in. But I've also seen the pleasure parents take from their children. I admit I haven't sought out contact with children, for example, babysitting for relatives or friends. I don't think anyone thinks of me as a babysitter candidate. If I had my own children, I'd do everything I could for them. Perhaps it would take some learning, but, if my relationship with you is any indication, contact with them would bring out feelings I can't conceive of at this point."

"That's fair, Archie. I have seen what appear to be instinctual demonstrations of affection for me that couldn't be learned. So perhaps it simply takes a trigger to remove barriers to those emotions in you."

"Well," said Archie. "If it requires a trigger, you've certainly pulled that trigger."

"That's enough for me for now," Nikki said. "I think you've answered my question."

Chapter 36

"Erasmus has come up with something on the hack attacks," Archie said as they reviewed evidence later. "Michalopoulos may have the skills to steal the credit card data from Hoskins' company, Involvement.com, particularly since security wasn't strong there. The denial-of-service attack, however, usually requires more of an organization that can activate a lot of computers simultaneously to simulate legitimate access to a service, but overwhelm it with volume. So I asked Erasmus to look at similarities of the denial-of-service attack on Involvement.com and other denial-of-service attacks to see if he could identify any patterns that would lead to a group capable of helping Michalopoulos do this. He found with relative certainty that it was a group in Russia. He used his strongest resources to see if he could find a connection between Michalopoulos and this group."

Nikki knew what those "strongest resources" were.

Archie continued. "Michalopoulos' work at the security firm made him aware of such groups, including the ones that did it as a business. Apparently his firm even paid some of these groups to guarantee they wouldn't hack customers of the firm. So he probably knew how to contact them. Erasmus found some communications between Michalopoulos and this group using a new e-mail account he set up. He tried to hide his connection to the account, but Erasmus' resources found the connection. All this probably isn't enough for legal action under the US Computer Fraud and Abuse Act."

"Particularly since some of the proof came through channels you can't admit to," Nikki said.

"Yes," Archie said. "But I can express it to the FBI as suspicions, pointing them in the right direction, and hope they have similar resources."

"Well, it can't hurt if you express it carefully. And they may be able to use their knowledge of the organization that he used in the denial-of-service attack to bluff having more proof. I hope all this cumulative evidence helps get a deal that puts him away for a long time."

Archie nodded. "If he is the murderer, and we can't prove it, at least the murder led to evidence of other crimes that will get him some punishment."

Chapter 37

Nikki and Archie's relationship continued to evolve positively, with them spending more time—and more evenings—together at one or the other's place. Nikki marveled at how they seemed to always have something to talk about or do together that they both enjoyed. At the same time, they could be together and relax separately, for example, reading books or news magazines or, in Nikki's case, checking social media. On the occasions that weren't the best, such as a movie that disappointed them, they seemed to agree on the disappointment. Even those occasions brought them closer.

Perhaps it's human nature to be skeptical when things are going well, particularly if the history of such relationships in the past suggested they were in fact too good to be true. Nikki still had some concerns about not being isolated socially. She arranged a dinner with a former roommate from college and her husband at her place, both because she owed them an invitation and because she wanted to reassure herself of Archie's improved social skills.

Archie tended to look at things analytically. It was strange for him to have feelings he couldn't explain with logic. But he certainly had those feelings for Nikki. Some of the feelings he understood came from the pleasure of sex, and he had experienced some of those feelings with other women—at least in the form of wanting to be with them again. But, in those other cases, the drive was largely sexual. In retrospect, he realized he tolerated the social aspects of those involvements for the sex; he felt he was working at the relationship. With Nikki, the social relationship developed before the sex, and he enjoyed being with her even before their relationship changed. Archie realized that he was experiencing what all the movies and novels called "love," and he liked it. Even trying to be more social for the sake of the relationship wasn't proving to be a task; he liked the reaction his more social stance created in others. From a purely rational point of view, it could even aid his detective work. And he'd always enjoyed mastering a new skill.

Nikki explained the couple coming to dinner to Archie the day before the guests arrived. "They are Alice and Tom Weinstein. Alice was my roommate for a couple of years in college, and we've kept in touch. She got married shortly after college, but it didn't work out. She just married Tom a couple of years ago, after they lived together for a while. Alice is a journalist at the *LA Times*. She generally does articles on local political figures and controversies. Tom is an electrical engineer, working for a defense contractor."

She cooked salmon with just lemon and pepper, and served it with a salad and rice. "I can cook more fancy dishes," she explained apologetically to Archie before the guests arrived. "But I didn't want to get too involved in the kitchen and miss a chance to talk."

Nikki had maintained a friendship with Alice, occasionally meeting her for lunch, but hadn't yet revealed the change in her relationship with Archie, perhaps revealing her remaining level of caution. Alice knew, of course, of her professional relationship with Archie. Nikki thought about telling Alice of the deeper relationship before the dinner, but decided to just let things evolve.

Archie brought a couple of bottles of wine that Erasmus indicated got good reviews. When Alice and Tom arrived, introductions were made, and they sat at the table. Archie poured the wine, having studied dinner manners through Erasmus. He decided he should take the role of co-host. As he did so, Nikki realized that Archie might be assuming the guests knew about the closer relationship; she hadn't told him otherwise.

Alice had a surprise, which came out in initial conversations revolving around "what's new." "I'm pregnant," she said with a smile. "That's new." Tom beamed—he did, of course, have a role in this announcement.

"Wow!" Nikki said. "Congratulations!"

"Tom and I are both busy," Alice said. "And we were putting it off until we thought we had more time, but realized that we had to make time for a child. And we will."

"Having a child is a big responsibility," Tom said. "It is obviously a bigger burden on the woman than the man, but I intend to help however I can."

Archie wasn't sure how to react. Erasmus hadn't covered this possibility. So he mimicked Nikki. "Congratulations." He added, trying to come up with something more, "It will be a great contribution to the genetic pool."

Tom and Alice laughed. Alice said, "We take that as a compliment."

Nikki said, smiling, "Leave it to Archie to think of the bigger picture. Your contribution to mankind."

Archie was emboldened by his apparent successful reaction to the news. "Nikki and I discussed having children."

There was silence around the table. Archie realized something was wrong, but wasn't sure what he should do.

Finally, Alice said, "Nikki, you apparently haven't told me everything about your relationship with Archie!"

Nikki said, "I didn't tell Archie that you didn't know we had gotten romantically involved. It's relatively recent. The discussion we had about children was obviously in the abstract."

Archie realized his mistake. "I'm sorry," he said. "I didn't realize you didn't know we had a relationship beyond work."

"Don't be sorry," Alice said. "I'm ecstatic! I've hoped Nikki would find someone, and I wondered why this didn't happen sooner, to be honest. She always spoke of you admiringly," she said to Archie. "I hope you two eventually contribute to the genetic pool."

That broke the tension. Everyone laughed.

"Well," Nikki said. "I guess you now know Archie better. He isn't always subtle."

"I love it," Tom said. "I hope you two will always feel you don't have to be subtle with us. It's another compliment that you told us, even if the revelation was unintentional."

Archie was still uncomfortable that he had stumbled, afraid that Nikki would interpret it as a social failure of the type she feared. "I love her," he said. "It's hard for me not to show it."

Nikki looked at Archie, and tears seemed to come to her eyes. Alice said, "That's beautiful, Archie."

"I guess I should respond," Nikki said. "But that leaves me speechless. It's early in our relationship, but it's been wonderful. I don't want to respond with a cliché. Archie is unique, as I hope you can see, and I am beginning to learn to embrace that uniqueness." She realized that Archie would never be perfect socially, but suddenly understood that was part of what she loved about him. Archie would always be Archie.

Despite the clumsiness of the revelation, the aftermath brought a level of intimacy to the rest of the evening. Discussion turned to many other subjects, including a brief discussion of the current investigation. Tom explained his current project at work, and Archie's ability to comprehend the technical description and ask intelligent questions about it brought the two of them closer.

The evening ended with hugs. "Next time, our house," Alice said.

Chapter 38

After Alice and Tom left, Archie said, "I'm sorry I blurted out something I should have kept private." He was still worried, despite the pleasant evening, that his blunder would hurt their relationship.

Nikki took Archie in her arms and gave him a passionate kiss. "Archie, I owe you an apology. If I love you, I have to accept an occasional social stumble. It's part of you. In some ways, I guess, it's part of your charm. I've been creating an artificial hurdle for you, and I appreciate your trying to jump it. The point, I realize, is that you make the effort, and you've been remarkably successful. But, if someone doesn't accept you as you are, that's their problem."

She pulled back and looked at him sincerely. "I love you." Perhaps she was fully admitting it to herself for the first time. "I guess everyone has a different interpretation of what that means. What it means to me is that you add immeasurably to my life, and I'd like this connection to continue for the rest of my life. Maybe that's idealistic, but I'd like to give it a try."

"I'd like to give it a try as well," Archie said. "For the rest of my life."

Chapter 39

The search warrant was granted on Dolores Hoskins' house. Nikki and Archie went there with the forensics team.

They searched for the obvious things, such as a gun, or incriminating notes, not really expecting to find anything in those categories. The key target was any digital communications they could find from any other smartphones, tablets, or PCs in the house. The technicians collected files from PCs, and Archie did his own collection, connecting Erasmus to any such devices through his smartphone.

They waited for Erasmus' initial results. "One new item has the highest correlation with the Hoskins murder," Erasmus reported. "Prior to the murder, she contacted Edward Hoskins' primary physician. Then, a cancer specialist Hoskins was seeing. Names and contact information of doctors sent to smartphone."

"It's interesting that she would contact *his* doctors during a divorce proceeding," Nikki said. She and Archie set out immediately for the office of the primary physician, Alfred Knox. They had to wait 15 minutes, but he agreed to see them briefly when they told the receptionist is was the police in regard to the murder of one of his patients.

"I suspect you are here about Edward Hoskins," he said when they were ushered into his office. "I view patient confidentiality as sacred, even after they are dead," he said.

"We know about his cancer from the autopsy," Nikki said. "And, if you view patient confidentiality so highly, why did you tell his wife about his condition?"

Knox looked surprised. "I felt I could discuss his case with his wife, of course," he said.

"A wife in the final stages of divorce," Archie said.

Knox raised his eyebrows. "I didn't know that."

"I'm sure she didn't want you to. She had a multi-million dollar life insurance policy on him."

"Well," he said nervously, "all I told her is to talk to Abe Hahn, his cancer physician."

"Indirectly telling her he had cancer," Nikki pointed out.

"That's your interpretation," Knox said defensively. "I have a backlog of patients. I don't wish to talk further."

Chapter 40

They headed to the office of Abraham Hahn. Again, the statement of the need to talk to the doctor about a murdered patient got them in for what they assured would be a brief discussion.

Hahn hadn't made the connection when they came in. "My assistant said that you were here about the murder of one of my patients. Who is that?"

"You haven't heard about the murder of Edward Hoskins?" Nikki asked.

"Oh, yes, it was in all the papers."

"We know he was seeing you about the pancreatic cancer our pathologist found, and had little time to live," Archie said, getting to the point and avoiding the patient confidentiality bit.

Hahn nodded hesitantly, indirectly validating that his assessment was consistent with the pathologist's.

"And we know you gave his wife the same information," Nikki added.

He nodded again.

"How long did you tell her he had to live?" Archie said.

Hahn finally spoke up. "Just a few months, as you said."

"What else did you tell her?" Nikki probed.

"I'm not sure I should tell you," Hahn said.

"She's not a patient, is she?" Archie asked.

"No."

Nikki looked impatient. "If we have to get a warrant to find out what you told her, we're going to ask a lot more questions, including why you would even talk to a wife near the end of a divorce proceeding."

"What!" Hahn exclaimed. "She didn't tell me that!"

"And you didn't ask," Nikki continued. "What else did you tell her?"

Hahn was flustered. "I just said that I was concerned he was considering suicide."

"Why?"

"He made some sort of statement like, 'So there isn't much reason to go through all the pain then, is there?'"

"You had told him to expect pain?" Archie asked.

"It's obvious. I said he'd have to be in the hospital with heavy pain medication in the final stages. I must be honest with my patients."

They talked a bit further, but nothing else of interest was unearthed.

Chapter 41

"Does this eliminate the wife as a suspect?" Nikki asked as they left the doctor's office. "She knew he'd be dead within a few months from the cancer or even his own hand. Why murder him?"

Archie thought. "Erasmus, do you have a copy of the life insurance policy of Edward Hoskins?"

"Yes, from the early investigation," Erasmus replied.

"Does it mention suicide?" Archie asked.

"Yes. There is a suicide exemption. The policy doesn't pay if he kills himself."

"Ahh…" Nikki said. "Murder to prevent suicide!"

"I'd say this shores up the case against the wife a bit, since we have witnesses to her curiosity about Hoskins' health and her knowledge of a possible suicide through the cancer specialist."

"But not even enough evidence for an arrest," Nikki said. "Her alibi stood up, so we'd have to find who might have done it and how she contacted the killer."

"Or find out who she contacted that might be the killer. Checking the divorce lawyer connection didn't lead anywhere."

Archie raised his smartwatch to his mouth. "Erasmus, what contacts from Dolores Hoskins occurred after her visit to the cancer doctor. Rank highest those contacts that were less frequent prior to the appointment."

"Checking contacts after visit to Abraham Hahn on Dolores Hoskins' calendar. Ranking based on newness. Verify."

"Yes," Archie confirmed.

"List of calls, texts, and e-mails sent to smartphone, with links to contents."

Archie perused the list. "It looks as if most contacts were with people she contacted regularly. Erasmus, on the top-ranked names on the last list, do any messages mention a meeting?"

"Three do. Flagged on your list."

Archie reviewed the three messages. "Nothing here that seems suspicious. She has a hair appointment at a salon. Long shot, but maybe the stylist has a boyfriend or friend that she told Dolores isn't too nice at a previous visit."

"Not that it's my thing," Nikki said, "but stylists often like to pass the time with 'interesting' conversation, so it's a possibility."

Chapter 42

Nikki decided she needed her hair trimmed, so she went to the stylist "undercover." Erasmus had given her background on the stylist, Amy Smith. Smith had divorced a fellow who had a criminal record, although they were petty thefts, not violent crimes. She was living with someone who seemed unremarkable, an average guy with an average job and no criminal record.

Despite Smith's prices being well above Nikki's usual range, Nikki went through with the hair appointment (wondering if she could write it off as a business expense). In initial conversations with Smith, Nikki said she was a physical trainer, something she had actually done as a part-time job in college. When Amy asked how Nikki had found her, Nikki said that Dolores Hoskins had recommended her, describing her as a former fitness student that had become a friend.

"Dolores was here fairly recently," Amy said. "As you know, she's going through a divorce."

"Well," Nikki said. "I guess she doesn't have to worry about that now."

"Why is that?" Amy asked.

"Her husband was murdered."

Amy appeared surprised. "I hadn't heard about that."

"It was in all the papers," Nikki said.

"I don't read the papers much," Amy said. "Do they know who did it?"

"No," Nikki said. "It's a bit strange. He was dying from cancer, so I don't understand why anyone would kill him."

"What did Dolores say about it?" Amy asked.

"I got the impression that it simplified her life. She didn't seem too broken up."

"Well," Amy said, "that's understandable. They were going through a divorce. That doesn't usually mean a warm relationship."

"Well," Nikki replied, "he did support her well for a long time. I get the impression she was more motivated by financial considerations to divorce him than any personal animosity."

"I guess," Amy said. "She told me she wasn't going to get much out of the divorce proceedings because he was having money problems. She did know about the cancer, and was delaying the divorce proceedings."

"Why?" Nikki asked.

"Because there was a life insurance policy with her as a beneficiary. She was making sure the premiums were paid."

"Did she say anything else about the insurance?" Nikki asked innocently.

"Well, she was a bit cynical, I guess. She said his doctor said he might consider suicide, so she was hoping that she would get the money sooner than waiting till he died from natural causes."

Nikki was surprised. "I thought life insurance policies didn't pay in the case of suicide."

"Really? Then she would have been in for a big surprise. She seemed to be hoping that he would commit suicide."

Nikki thought that this could either be a clever ruse by Dolores, or a protective fabrication by Amy. But it certainly didn't bolster the case against Dolores. She decided to probe Amy's connections to someone who might have been involved. "You said a divorce doesn't lead to a warm relationship. Have you been through one?"

"Unfortunately, yes. I married a 'tough' guy. He was macho, or so I thought. He'd even been in jail. I guess when you're young, that type of thing seems masculine. But it's stupid. Guys like that are impossible to live with."

"Was he still into crime?"

"No, he got a factory job. But he continually had to show he was tough, partly by being abusive."

"Physically abusive?

"No, verbally, but he'd act as if he could back it up physically. I ended up hating the guy."

"Do you have any contact with him now?"

"No, we live far enough apart that I don't even see him on the street. And if I did, I'd walk the other direction." Amy sounded angry even thinking about seeing him. "Now, I'm living with what you might call a 'nice guy.' He shows me he cares for me, and even does a little cooking. And, the funny thing is, I even enjoy the sex more because it's obvious he prizes sleeping with me, and wouldn't cheat on me. He's even changed me. I appreciate tenderness over false macho stuff." Amy seemed to be tearing up. "He's the kind of guy I could imagine having children with."

"That's wonderful, Amy," Nikki said. But she didn't feel wonderful herself. This conversation seemed to be closing doors in the investigation, rather than opening them.

She decided to try one direct probe. "Does your old boyfriend hire out to intimidate people, or have a friend that does? I have an old boyfriend myself that I think is stalking me, and I'd like someone to frighten him off."

"I don't think he would do anything like that. He's never been involved in anything violent. He talks the game, but doesn't play it. And the stint in jail scared the shit out of him. He plays it straight. I wouldn't have got involved with him in the first place if he was still a criminal or hanging out with them. I was stupid, but not that stupid."

Nikki did get a nice hairdo out of the encounter, but nothing more.

Chapter 43

Nikki had surreptitiously recorded the conversation, and Erasmus transcribed it for the record and so that Archie could review it quickly. He did.

"Dolores knew about Hoskins' illness. If she really thought the policy covered suicide, she has no motive."

"Yes," Nikki said. "But she could have reviewed the policy more closely after her conversation with Amy."

"Well, even so," Archie said. "If Amy is being honest, she didn't have anyone to suggest to Dolores to do the deed. We should double check the ex-husband's whereabouts at the time of the murder if we can, just to be sure." He asked Erasmus to see if the fellow had used his credit card that evening as a first check. Erasmus indicated that that he couldn't provide an immediate answer.

While Nikki and Archie were reviewing the murder case and not getting anywhere, Erasmus sounded an alarm. Archie had asked him to monitor Michalopoulos' activities. He indicated that Michalopoulos had bought an airline ticket with an ultimate destination of Croatia, which doesn't have an extradition treaty with the US, and was transferring large sums of money to banks in Croatia.

Archie quickly sent a message to the FBI about Michalopoulos' apparent plan to flee. His contact quickly acknowledged the message and said he would process it with "utmost priority."

Later that day, Archie received the notification that Michalopoulos would be arrested shortly by local FBI agents on a number of charges, including the credit card theft. But not murder.

Chapter 44

The FBI reported later that they had indeed arrested Michalopoulos as he was packing, and some of the things he was packing, including documentation of off-shore accounts they hadn't yet found, strengthened their case. They also arrested Fred Oberteuffer, Michalopoulos' partner-in-crime at National Security Solutions, at the same time, having previously negotiated a deal where Oberteuffer got a break on charges for testifying against Michalopoulos.

"They say that the case against Michalopoulos is very strong," Archie reported to Nikki.

"It's still unsatisfying not to know if he was the murderer, even if he'll be in jail for a long time."

"At this point," Archie replied, "we should just view it as one case solved. We still have an open murder investigation."

"The only remaining suspect with a motive is the wife, although her alibi suggests she would have had to hire someone to do it."

Archie asked Erasmus for an update on the stylist's ex-husband. Erasmus replied, "He used his credit card at a gas station between work and home that night. See map."

Archie pulled his smartphone from his pocket and studied it. "His home is in the opposite direction from his work as Hoskins' house. So it doesn't appear he is the killer. He could have possibly made it in time if he turned around and went to Hoskins' house immediately, but why go so far out of his way if that was his intention?"

"To create an alibi, perhaps," Nikki speculated. "To be able to claim he was at home, even if there are no witnesses to that fact."

"I guess we have to see what he says," Archie concluded.

Chapter 45

They went to Wells' house that evening. He was home, and seemed more annoyed than alarmed when they introduced themselves as the police. "What the hell? Just because I made a few mistakes in the past doesn't mean you can harass me forever."

"We don't believe you did anything wrong, Mr. Wells," Nikki said reassuringly, "but your name came up in an investigation, and we have to follow up."

"My name came up? In what kind of investigation?" Wells said.

"Murder," Archie said.

Wells went pale. "What the hell? What are you talking about?"

Fear apparently made him more cooperative. They asked about the night in question, and it took him a moment to think back. "That was a workday. I just went home that night to watch the basketball game with my friend Nick."

"What game was on that night?" Archie asked.

"Clippers versus Rockets."

"Who won?"

"The Clippers, with a last-minute basket."

Archie asked Erasmus for the game that night and the score. He confirmed Wells' recollection. Wells provided contact info for Nick, and Nick later confirmed by phone that he had watched the game with Wells.

After that confirmation, Nikki said, "This could all be a plan to have an alibi, perhaps, with cooperation of a friend or even an accomplice, but it seems real."

Archie checked out what Erasmus could find out about the friend's whereabouts that evening. Nick had made a mobile phone call from Wells' house near the time of the murder, so it appeared that both had relatively solid alibis.

Chapter 46

It was a frustrating day, with clues that led nowhere. They went to Archie's house after work to have a light dinner and a couple of glasses of wine. They determined not to talk business that night. They shopped online for some cooking utensils Archie needed. "You know," Archie said, "if we lived together, we could share things. We wouldn't have to support two households."

"That's another level of commitment," Nikki said, not commenting on the obvious invitation that Archie had issued. "We do spend almost every evening together now, and I must admit, I do feel something is missing when we aren't together. But, if we lived together, we'd have to give each other space to be alone occasionally, to work on hobbies or read. I don't want us to feel we have to constantly give each other attention. I suspect that is what hurts a lot of relationships. And we're both used to a lot of time alone."

"I understand what you are saying. We've talked about this before, and I agree one hundred percent," Archie said. "Just being sensitive to that issue will help. And, if you move in here, there is room for you to have a separate office from my home office—a bit of a retreat. If you are in there with the door closed, I'll honor your privacy."

"And I can do the same for you. And, if either of us has to go out for errands or meetings separately, we shouldn't have to report constantly."

Archie replied, "But we have dangerous jobs, so we should be conscious of not causing needless worry by not letting the other know when one's schedule varies significantly."

"Good point," Nikki said. "I guess there's a balance. Will you tell me when you visit your girlfriend?"

Archie looked puzzled, not getting the joke. "You're my girlfriend."

Nikki smiled. "I'm glad you understand that."

Archie got it. "As long as we're together, you don't have to worry about that. It's more likely that you'll get plenty of attention from my competitors."

"My ego isn't so insecure that I'd react to attention. I promise you, Archie, I won't react inappropriately to that attention as long as we're together. And, for that matter, you're likely to get some attention yourself."

"Are we agreeing that you'll move in with me?" Archie said.

"We're agreeing I'll think about it for a few days. And you can change your mind in the interim if you wish."

Chapter 47

At work the next day, they expressed their frustration with having nothing further to pursue in the murder investigation. "We've dug as deep as we can with our two current suspects. Should we look for other suspects? It could have even been a random burglary, with the burglar getting in under some artifice."

Archie looked as if he had a revelation. "We do have another suspect that we may have eliminated too soon."

Nikki was surprised. "And who is that?"

"Hoskins himself. The doctor said he was contemplating suicide, and he made that comment to the bankruptcy lawyer about what would happen next. And, with a painful death approaching and no money to make his final days more pleasant, no children and no wife, suicide might have been attractive to him."

"But there was no gun at the scene," Nikki said.

"We should examine the evidence skeptically, as we always do, and see how that could be," Archie said. "Erasmus, did Hoskins own a gun?"

After a short pause, Erasmus said, "There is a handgun registered in his name, registered more than a year ago."

"And we didn't find it during the search of his house," Nikki said. "Perhaps we should look for a place he might hide it."

"If it was for protection, it wouldn't be too well hidden, or it would be hard to get to in a hurry."

Nikki was skeptical. "But why would he stage a suicide to look like a murder?"

Archie looked as if he'd just had an inspiration. "To get us to investigate Michalopoulos for murder, and look for a motive, which Hoskins conveniently provided on a poorly protected PC. He didn't have the resources to prove his suspicions, but perhaps he thought law enforcement might."

Nikki went along with the train of thought. "And he drew Michalopoulos to his house so that Michalopoulos wouldn't have an alibi."

"And turned off the surveillance camera that showed Michalopoulos never came in the house!" Archie said excitedly.

Nikki looked puzzled. "But why would he attempt to crawl toward the side table with the phone on it. And why shoot himself in the stomach, a slow and painful death, instead of the head?"

"It wasn't painful, with the overdose of pain pills he took," Archie said. "Perhaps he wanted to die slowly for some reason. Perhaps to get rid of the gun and make it look like murder."

"But why would he try to crawl toward the phone on the side table if he wanted to die? And where is the gun? It just doesn't hold together."

Archie looked startled. "The drawer on the side table was empty!"

"So?"

"Do you have any empty drawers in your place?" Archie asked excitedly.

"No, I guess not. I see why that might be unusual, but where does it take us?"

"I remember thinking that the drawer was very shallow, and that might explain why he didn't use it. But I didn't realize the implication of that."

Nikki was still puzzled. "I don't understand what you're saying."

"I can tell you exactly where the gun is!" Archie exclaimed. "Is our search warrant still current?"

"Yes, since the house was going to be vacant, I left time to revisit it. And we've preserved the crime scene. That wasn't a problem, since there was a bankruptcy process that hasn't played out, and the house is an asset."

"Let's go there now!" Archie insisted.

"OK," Nikki said, "I guess you want to keep me in suspense."

"I could be wrong, but we'll know soon."

Chapter 48

They went to Hoskins' house with a technician, whom they asked to record their activities with a video and take any evidence they might find. They went to the living room where Hoskins' body was found.

Archie said, "Begin recording. Note the blood trail to the side table."

He put on a rubber glove. "The table has a drawer." He opened the drawer.

"It appears empty. But note how shallow it is. Shallower than the depth of the drawer on the outside."

Nikki raised her eyebrows in surprise. She realized what Archie was getting at.

They asked the technician to pry off the apparent floor of the drawer while Archie did the video recording. He did so carefully. The floor didn't come up easily; it was obviously glued down. But it gave eventually, revealing...

"Aha!" Archie said. "Case closed!"

There was a gun under the apparent bottom of the drawer. The board plied away was a false bottom that had been glued to some wooden supports on the sides of the drawer.

"I suspect we'll find that this is the gun that shot Hoskins, and that the blood on it is his. The powder residue the medical examiner found on his right hand is further confirmation that he shot himself."

"He deliberately shot himself in a way that gave him time to put the gun in the hidden compartment." Nikki said. "Unbelievable. It was a suicide."

"And it looks like he put wet glue on the fake bottom before shooting himself and held it open with that wad of paper next to the gun until he put the gun in and pressed the bottom down."

"We never really looked for a way he could have faked suicide initially, because we didn't have any reason to think he'd gain anything by staging what looked like a murder."

"It probably shouldn't have taken us this long to discover the ruse," Archie said.

"We wouldn't have at all if you hadn't looked into that drawer," Nikki said. "Give yourself some credit. But what is the crushed paper? Is it just something random?"

Archie carefully removed it and opened it. He nodded as he read it. "It's a note from Hoskins. It says, 'I guess you discovered my little trick. But I hope you get that bastard Michalopoulos.'"

The tech said, "I'll bag all this. You guys are amazing. Congratulations."

Nikki said as they walked to the car, "Well, the end of one adventure. But the beginning of another. I'll move in with you, Archie. What we have is too good not to test further."

Archie beamed. "And they lived happily ever after."

"That remains to be seen. But we'll definitely see."